Aggressive Optimism

By

Jenna Edwards

Publishing Services provided by Paper Raven Books LLC
Printed in the United States of America
First Printing, 2023

Paperback ISBN= 978-1-962897-02-0
Hardback ISBN= 978-1-962897-03-7

TRIGGER WARNING

In the pages ahead, you will encounter a vivid portrayal of a harrowing car crash that leads to the loss of lives and delves into the emotional aftermath of trauma and post-traumatic stress disorder (PTSD). The scenes are intended to evoke intense emotions and explore the complexities of human experiences in the face of tragedy.

The narrative will explore the psychological and emotional impact that such events can have on individuals and their loved ones. It will delve into themes of grief, survivor's guilt, and the challenging journey towards healing and recovery.

Remember that your mental and emotional health are important. If you choose to continue reading, consider reaching out to a supportive friend, family member, or mental health professional to discuss your feelings as needed. It's important to engage with the material in a way that feels comfortable and safe for you.

Ultimately, this novel aims to explore the depth of human resilience and the transformative power of empathy and support. Thank you for your understanding and consideration as you embark on this emotional journey.

To the love of my life—thanks for proving you're with me even when the wheels fall off.

Chapter One

My voice finds the perfect note, the one I've worked so hard to achieve, and I know in an instant I actually, amazingly, got it right. I can't believe it. But, almost immediately, doubt creeps in, and I start to second-guess myself. Did I really just do it, or am I imagining it like I have every day since I got the solo? There's a moment of silence, and then applause thunders through my feet as the stage shakes from the vibration. Half the town is here. I swallow hard. As the adrenaline fades and nausea threatens to take over. Do not throw up! Do not throw up! These words become my mantra. I know my cheeks must be a bright red because I can feel the heat reaching up from my neck. A nervous sweat breaks out in a gush, and I hope it doesn't soak through my dress. My mom and I spent hours shopping for this dress and spent way more money than we should have, just so I would feel confident standing on this old rickety wooden stage. But I definitely don't feel confident. I feel exposed. The sweat beads on my forehead. I remember to graciously accept the applause, as Mrs. M, our choir teacher, told me to do, but I feel dizzy.

I manage to bow without falling over or throwing up. Success! When I straighten, I catch a glimpse of my friends in the crowd. Their giant, beaming smiles are filled with an embarrassing amount of pride because they know how hard I worked to perfect my solo. They also know about my dream of becoming a professional singer. *Oh gosh, is my smile as silly as theirs right now?* I check in with my face. No, it's the appropriate amount of smile. *Okay, time to walk back to your place with the others.* I make my way back to the risers.

I have dreamed about moving to Hollywood and becoming a famous singer for as long as I can remember, so I lucked out when I moved to Karlville a few years ago. Because, even though the town is basically the epitome of a locker room and wouldn't know a Shakespearean verse if the man himself rose from the dead and put on a play right in front of them with flashing lights saying, "Shakespeare play here!" they do have one of the best show choirs in the entire state.

Choir in our school, though completely underfunded, is sort of like a team sport. We began rehearsals before school even started so we could be ready for the homecoming concert. Though it cut the summer before my senior year short, it feels great to be this prepared just weeks after school started.

We are a nationally ranked choir, and that is all thanks to our fearless leader, Mrs. M. She grew up in our small town and came back here to whip our choir into shape immediately after her college graduation. She is something of a legend. A bit intimidating, but warm as well. Sort of like that aunt who is surprisingly fun, but only if you do the dishes without being asked. Her choir direction is unparalleled, and I can't believe how good it feels to be reaping the rewards.

I admire her, and so, I do my best to follow her direction, which includes the whole "taking a compliment with grace" thing. I wish it was easier and am now wondering if I did it right. I'll just ask her after the show. But I know that if I want to be a professional singer, I need to do so much more than learn how to take a compliment. *How can I want to be famous so badly and yet be so embarrassed and insecure whenever anyone even notices me, let alone gives me praise?* I walk the short distance back to the risers. It feels like a thousand miles. Mrs. M beams and gives a nod of approval. She's happy with how I received the applause.

I carefully make my way to the top and settle back into my place amongst the choir, thinking, *Okay, you're good.* As I double-check that my feet are firmly planted on the riser, it wobbles below the weight of all thirty of us as we crescendo to the end of the song. I know it doesn't make sense. I feel unbelievably conflicted and unable to express what that feels like to anyone, so I just sit with the emotions, hoping to work them out so I can live my dream.

More applause shakes the stage and threatens to topple the risers over as I look up toward the spotlight. I can just make out my family. My little sister, Jane, is sitting next to my mom and dad, who are both blocked equally by the light, so I see the left half of my mom and the right half of my dad as they maneuver the heavy spotlight. They are running the lights, and my little sister is enjoying the show, no doubt. While I hope that's the case for them all, I don't anticipate they understand what a big moment that was for me. I imagine they are beaming with pride. Mom and Dad are actual rock musicians, so performing comes super easy to them both. They have no idea what it's like to work for weeks on a single note, or what it's like to not know how to take a compliment or applause, for that matter. They're also two of the busiest people in the world so, unlike Jane, they haven't been tortured by my singing the one note over and over again until I got it right for the past three weeks. *Jane's probably glad that's over*, I think to myself as a little smirk crosses my face.

My parents being in a rock band definitely causes some problems with the local town folk (as I like to call them because I swear they all still live in the 1950s), but right now, I'm so grateful they are here, helping with the lights and watching me live a tiny part of my dream.

We start singing the next song, and I think, "Thank god for them," as the lights change colors, making everyone on stage feel like they're in a real pro production. My parents are feeling the love, and I am beaming with pride to have them. This is their element, and I am grateful they're giving their time and expertise. *Maybe it will buy us some favor with the town.* We sway from left to right, singing our hearts out. *Oh, who am I kidding? History has shown we'll never be accepted here, so just get over it.*

Also, who needs 'em, anyway? In 159 days, I'll be done and on my way to Hollywood. My parents are the only reason I feel like there's any hope for me to live my dreams, even though I feel completely trapped by my surroundings. I'm super happy they're so supportive, but I still have to fight some serious resentment towards them because I absolutely hate this place, and they're the reason I have to be in this small-minded, backwards-thinking town. But I digress.

Right now, all I want to do is enjoy the moment and be happy they're here. Gotta find the positive in all situations, right?

As the choir sings the last song, our voices meld like one, in a rising crescendo. The crowd's energy is palpable. My skin thrums with nervous energy and excitement. I can't believe I just started my senior year with a standing ovation!

After the concert finishes and the big, blue velvet curtain falls, I immediately make my way to the back of the stage. I join my two best friends, waiting for me. They're wearing identical embarrassing smiles. I wave and begin to take a step down when BAM! A freshman stagehand takes a dive and falls flat on his face, right in front of me. Clearly, his glasses, which are now halfway across the stage, are not working. *Don't laugh! Don't laugh!* I will myself not to bust into a gut-belly laugh because I can see how embarrassed he feels. So, instead, I feel awful for even thinking about laughing as I help him up. His face is as red as I imagine mine was a few minutes ago.

"Thank you." His voice wobbles as much as his feet as he gains his composure.

"No problem," I say, looking at him with empathy.

He manages to smile. "You did a great job."

My face gets hot again, but I accept the compliment. "Thank you."

Just then Jessa, the bane of my existence, and daily tormentor, shoulder-checks me like a pro football player. I think she gets lessons from her annoyingly handsome jerk of a football player boyfriend, Chip. I try not to show how much it actually hurts. Her shoulders are insanely pointy.

"Oh, sweetie," she says with her seriously obnoxious, fake Southern drawl. "Oops. Didn't see you there."

Seriously, no one can figure out why she talks with a Southern accent since we live in the Midwest. But no one dares to question the queen bee for fear that they would be where I am, on her daily duplicitous to-do list. I honestly think she has one, and I wouldn't be surprised if it's actually written down:

- Biology Homework
- Buy Eye Shadow
- Choir Practice
- *Torment Nif*

YOU DID TOO SEE ME THERE! I scream in my head, but I force a, "No problem," out of my mouth as I grit my teeth, willing myself not to act on my impulse to punch her in the face since she *clearly* saw me there. Then I turn towards my friends, who just witnessed the whole thing.

"Fudge sticks," I say. I want to throw a massive f-bomb, but I heard my acting hero once explain that, "Swearing stifles an actor's ability to create. You must be able to find more articulate ways to express your feelings." She was right! It's really difficult to express yourself without swear words. And though my main goal in life is to be a famous singer, I think it's good advice for all performers, so I work with it.

My friends, Zane and Karsten, are silent. They just open their arms to me for a group hug. I always feel so safe in our group hugs. Karsten, in his always appropriately timed biting commentary, breaks the silence with, "Jessa is such a horrid human." Zane and I giggle.

"I just don't get why she hates me. We used to be friends."

"She's just jealous," Zane replies and then notices how uncomfortable that makes me. So she adds, "And there's nothing you can do about it. Like my grandma always says, 'Don't you dare dim your light so others won't feel threatened by it.'"

Karsten adds, "Yeah, before you moved to town, she was queen bee of the choir, and now she has some serious competition, and she doesn't know how to handle it."

Karsten has a way of pointing out the obvious in a really funny, snarky, and at times flamboyant and dramatic way. He's so good at seeing into people's souls and understanding their motivation.

I sigh and look around. "All I know is that I want to take in this night. I still can't believe I hit that note. It felt incredible." I spin around like Julie Andrews in *The Sound of Music*. Except I lose my balance and almost tip over.

We all laugh giant belly laughs and return to our group hug.

"I'm so stinking proud of you, Nif," Zane says in her strange and comforting, I'm-almost-a-monk, but still super cool, hippie-dippy way. Zane was actually born on a hippie commune, and though her family moved back to Karlville before she became one, I think the energy of her birthplace has stuck with her.

As is our tradition, when we've collectively decided a moment is worth celebrating, our group hug becomes a jumping circle as we hold onto each other and try not to conk each other's heads. As we do this, we don't even see the woman approaching, and she comes dangerously close to becoming a victim of conking herself.

Zane is the first to notice and stop jumping. She says, "Sneaking up on us is a good way to get run over. Apologies. Didn't see you there."

"Oh, no, I should know better than to interrupt a celebration, and a well-deserved one at that." Her already bright smile becomes luminous. "My name is Karen Kolby." She hands me her business card. "I'm a news anchor for…"

"Channel 11 News," I respond, trying to hold back my total shock and excitement. I love her and her show, but play it as cool as I can. I continue, "I know who you are."

"Oh great," she says with false modesty dripping from her mouth, "then you know about my weekly feature called 'Stars Among Us,' where I feature local talent who I feel could be huge stars in the future, and I'd love to feature you."

All I can do is nod, or I might lose my mind with excitement. I have dreamed of this exact moment since before I can remember. The moment when I would be discovered. I watch her show religiously, hoping and praying that she would, one day, discover me. And that day is today. *Do not freak out! Do not freak out!*

Zane elbows me back to reality, and I look over to see her and Karsten both looking at me with faces that scream, SAY SOMETHING!

"Oh wow," I respond, trying to keep my cool. "That would be great."

She just keeps smiling, and I think, *That would be great? Really?* I know I'm trying to keep my cool, but I should probably show some enthusiasm.

I correct myself. "What I mean is that would be really great. What an honor. Thank you."

She smiles. "Great! Okay, call the number on the card tomorrow morning, and they'll give you all the details. Looking forward to having you on the show. Really fantastic job tonight."

And with that, Karen Kolby, maker of dreams, makes her exit. As soon as she is no longer in sight, I turn to Karsten and Zane with my mouth open so wide with shock that an entire wasp nest could fit inside. I scream, "Whaaaaattttt waaaaaaassss thaaat?"

We all get back into our celebration circle positions, only this time the celebratory energy is higher than any of us have felt before. I take it in and think to myself, *Is this the moment my dreams start to come true?*

The moment is broken by the one and only Jessa, who overheard the whole thing and appears out of nowhere as if she's got some sort of "I live to ruin Nif's happiest moments" radar. She crosses her arms and looks me up and down.

"Who do you think you are? Do you really think anyone wants to hear your dumb, tone-deaf voice blaring through their television sets?"

It is as if she has pulled out a giant pin and just popped the massive happiness balloon I had built up around me. Then she turns on her heel, flips her hair in the most mean-girl cliché manner, and walks away.

Karsten and Zane look at me, then each other, then back at me again. They know I'm about to go into one of my defeated spirals and do their best to pull me back to the amazing moment before Jessa came in and ruined it.

"Ugh, her energy is so icky." Zane rolls her eyes.

Karsten adds, "Sweetie, she's just trying to make herself feel better because you beat her out for that solo and then totally nailed it. Don't let her get to you. Her behavior is all about her insecurities."

I know he is right, but it's really hard not to believe her. I mean, who *do* I think I am? Why would anyone want to hear me sing? Why is it that this dream I have is so hard to achieve? Honestly, most days, I'm pretty sure I'm not at all equipped to handle the fame and fortune I dream of having. But, when I decide to give up, something in my soul feels so empty, and I just keep coming back. That has to mean something, right? Maybe it means I'm delusional.

Zane and Karsten can obviously see the thoughts in my head because Zane interrupts them with, "You know, my nana always says that you have to focus on what you want. And, if what you want seems impossible, you have to focus on it even more. She calls it, 'aggressive optimism.'"

You'd think Zane's grandma was like an 800-year-old shaman sitting on top of a magical mountain somewhere. When, in reality, I think she's only in, like, her 50s. I know that's still old, but it's not as old as you would think by the way she talks. I love her grandma and try to take in all her wisdom, but it's hard. It's, like, what she says makes sense, but to put it in practice just doesn't seem possible for me. But, I gotta say, the term is really sitting with me. Aggressive optimism. It has a good ring.

"I'll have to think on that one, Zane." I giggle. We make eye contact, she throws her arms around me and Karsten, and the three of us walk out of the gym shoulder to shoulder like an impenetrable wall.

Chapter Two

My little sister, Jane, runs ahead to open the door, but, per usual, her awkward, 11-year-old feet are faster than the door, and she runs into it face-first. We all laugh because you would think that after doing that, oh, about a million times, she'd have learned by now. But, nope, she still does it almost every single time.

I walk past her looking down at her cute little button nose as she rubs it from the pain, pat her head sarcastically, and stick my tongue out at her.

"Mooooommm!" she whines. "Nif…"

"Are you okay?" Mom asks, interrupting her because she knows the answer is yes. We can all tell that it is really more her pride than her face that was hurt.

"Who wants ice cream?" Dad asks as if he is Ward Cleaver from that old black-and-white TV show, *Leave It to Beaver*.

"Duh, everyone does, Dad. That's a ridiculous question," I assert, already grabbing the bowls from the cupboard.

Jane noisily gets the spoons while Mom grabs the toppings. She sets each out on the counter like a buffet. There's hot fudge, chocolate syrup, butterscotch syrup, strawberry syrup, caramel, chocolate chips, white chocolate chips, butterscotch chips, peanuts, three kinds of sprinkles, whipped cream, and cherries. (Never forget the cherries!) Ice cream at our house is like a religion. I mean, it *is* Minnesota, and although Wisconsin may be the state famous for dairy, Minnesota provides some steep competition.

Sitting down to enjoy our masterpieces, I can see that my parents are beaming with pride.

"Nif, you did such a great job!" my mom exclaims with surprising enthusiasm. I pull back a little because she is normally so matter-of-fact about performing. I think this might be the first time I've ever seen her this excited about anything I've done. Her reaction to my reaction is to double down. "No, really. I know how hard you worked to find your voice in that solo, and your hard work paid off. I think the town is going to be talking about that solo for a really long time."

"I'm just glad you were there tonight. Thank you both so much for running the lights. I know Mrs. M and the rest of the choir really appreciated it," I say, immediately shifting the focus away from me. The lump in my throat gets bigger as I try not to cry. Having people talk about me just feels gross.

My mom lets out a heavy sigh, looks down at the ground, and I can see that she is disappointed that I changed the focus. Now I feel even worse. That's the curse/blessing of having parents who are actual rock stars. They know what it takes to be successful in show business. A business I have dreamed of being in since I was three years old. I remember the day when I was lying on the floor watching a musical on television so intently, with my head in my hands, and I got so inspired to be *in* the TV, singing these incredible songs. I walked into the kitchen in my little pink footie pajamas and declared with matter-of-fact confidence that I was going to sing on TV one day! Instead of exuding the confidence I had when I was three, here I sit, looking at the disappointment in my parents' eyes.

"It felt really good to accomplish my goal." This seems to be enough for my mom. She smiles and reaches her hands out to hold mine across the table. I try not to roll my eyes. Sometimes my mom can be so cheesy.

Instead of resisting, which is what my entire being wants to do, I give in and hold her hands as she breaks into the dreaded "I remember when you were just three years old…" story.

Both my dad and my sister groan as she continues. "What? I get to be proud of my baby."

We all laugh and take bites of our ice cream. I tip my head back as the cold, sweet nectar makes its way slowly down my throat. I'm enjoying this perfect moment when suddenly, I realize the time.

"Oh snap! It's 9:30. I've got to get ready for bed."

"It's Friday night," my dad says, followed by a, "Yeah, why are you going to bed so early on a weekend?" from my mom, and a "You're so lame," from my sister.

"I have to open the restaurant in the morning." I start clearing the bowls. "Jane, will you please do the dishes so we don't get ants?" I ask. She responds by dramatically throwing her arms in the air and slowly dragging her feet across the floor.

"I gueeeesssss. If I haaaave to," she whines.

I quickly walk to the bathroom as my parents make their way to their studio in the basement to practice some new songs for the gig they have coming up. This is their most creative time, and I've been listening to them play loud rock music late at night my whole life, so it's sort of like a lullaby at this point.

"Why can't you just believe the good things people say about you?" I ask my reflection, staring back at me fighting back tears. *Flipping crud!* I think angrily to myself. *You're never going to make your dreams come true or get the flip out of here, if you don't start figuring out how to step the F up!* I'm so spitting mad at myself at this point as I fall asleep to the sound of punishing drums and wailing guitars. I'm so grateful that the beat matches the anger I feel inside. I just want to cry.

Chapter Three

I'M BEAT. IT'S ONLY NOON, BUT I'VE ALREADY WORKED a full day at my fast food job. I smell like a French fry. I walk back to my house, but instead of going in, I stop at the end of my driveway. I take a deep breath of the chilly autumn air, and look at this little house we live in, and for a moment, I don't hate it.

The moment is ruined when a car full of classmates drives by. A caustic voice says, "Look at Nif. Her parents must be so high that she has to work to pay their bills." The rest of the kids in the car laugh as the car screams past me.

"Shake it off," I mumble to myself.

I walk in through the tiny entrance that also doubles as our laundry room. The house is quiet. No one in my house loves to do the laundry, so I make my way over the lofty piles of dirty clothes like an obstacle course that must be mastered in order to actually get inside.

I accidentally lose my balance, stumbling over one of the piles, and stub my toe on the darn washing machine. I don't know why my mom insists on separating the clothes into piles before we're even ready to do the laundry. It just makes it such a pain to get around, but she does, so it is what it is.

Stubbing my toe on the washing machine sent out an unintentional howl that seems to have alerted the family to my arrival, and they begin to make their way to the kitchen.

"Did you bring cinnamon rolls?" Jane asks while rubbing her sleepy eyes. The sound of her plaid, flannel slippers scrape as she walks across the floor toward the box I've left on the counter.

"Jane, it's noon! Are you just waking up?" I ask as if I don't already know the answer.

"Of course. I'm not going to wake up if no one else is awake. That would be lame."

Jane is currently obsessed with the word lame. Apparently, it was said by her *favorite* actor on her *favorite* TV show, so it is now her *favorite* word.

She opens the box and sucks in a huge breath of the aroma of cinnamon and sugar before grabbing one of the gooey treats and taking a huge bite.

Just then, my parents walk through the door, also still in their pajamas.

"Ooooh, you brought the rolls," my dad exclaims with the same kid-like excitement Jane just had.

I laugh. "I'm pretty sure if I didn't bring food home from work, we'd starve." I chuckle as my whole family grabs the breakfast I brought home for them and sits down.

"I smell. I'm going to take a shower. Then Zane and Karsten are coming over to help me pick out an outfit for Monday." I head toward the tiny lone bathroom in the house.

Half an hour later, I emerge from the bathroom feeling a lot less greasy. I can hear the sound of cartoons and my family's laughter echoing down the hallway. I glance into the kitchen and see frosting dripping from the counter. The place is a disaster, but I can't think about it right now. I have to figure out what I'm wearing on Monday.

I walk into my room and see Zane sitting crisscross-applesauce on the bed, her back super straight as if she's going to do a deep meditation. I follow her eyeline toward my closet and lock my eyes on clothes being thrown out like an 80s romcom. Karsten pokes his head out and says with dramatic flair, "Oh, Nif, good. Got your game face on? 'Cause this is not a drill, sweetie." I look over to Zane and roll my eyes in the most loving way. Karsten's ability to turn a stressful situation into something fun is unsurpassed. And, seeing as I was stressed to the point where I thought I was going to have a heart attack while I was in the shower, Karsten is literally saving my life right now.

"Ahhhhh, thanks for coming, you two! Karsten, what'd you get for me?" I ask.

A long forty minutes later, Karsten comes out of the closet holding a feather boa from last year's fabulous seventies-themed Halloween party. My parents throw one every year, and I usually pretend to be sick. But last year, I decided to just go with it and dressed up as David Bowie. My parents were so happy. I, on the other hand, felt so awkward and itchy. Polyester is no one's friend.

"Oh my gosh! Where did you even find that?" I ask.

"Darling," Karsten declares in his richest, snobbiest accent, "it was in your closet, where all the fabulous clothes are hiding."

He throws the boa over one shoulder, pivots on his foot, and pulls out a garment bag all in one fell swoop, like it's a dance routine he's rehearsed to perfection.

He carries the garment bag over to the bed as if he's ready to present it to the queen.

"Don't you remember what this is?" he questions, clearly reading the confused looks on both my and Zane's faces.

"Not at all." I'm truly baffled.

Karsten squeals with delight. He loves to surprise people with his brilliance. He unzips the bag to reveal the coolest, 70s-style mini dress with long bell sleeves in black with big yellow, orange, and brown polka dots.

"How did you even remember that was in there? I totally forgot I showed it to you," I say, stunned.

"Listen, honey, this guy knows fashion, and this dress is pure fashion and completely unforgettable," he responds.

"I can't wear that; it's too loud. Right?" I look to Zane to back me up, but she's not having it.

"Sorry, Nif, I'm squarely on 'Team Karsten' on this one. This dress is perfect."

"No. No way. I could never pull this off. I don't have the right body type, the skirt is too short, it's so bright and bold. I just can't."

"All I'm hearing are excuses. And not even good ones at that. Go put it on." Zane sings his response.

Chapter Four

GOOD OLD JOAN JETT IS BLARING FROM THE SPEAKERS of my little yellow VW Bug, reminding me to get back on my feet again as I make my way the thirty miles to the nearest city—I use the word city loosely because in reality it's just a big town that happens to have a mall and be where the TV station is.

Singing alone at the top of my lungs in my car is one of the greatest joys of my life. I feel free, safely surrounded by the sentiments I am able to express through singing. It's the only time I truly feel like I can be myself.

This song in particular means a lot to me. My mom sings it in the band now, but when I was little, right after my mom divorced my biological dad, we would put this song on and dance around the living room singing into our hairbrushes. We'd play air guitar and jump up on the couch, pretending it was a platform on a stage. It was a really difficult time in our lives, but music brought us together. That's what inspired me to be a singer. The way the lyrics made me feel in my heart and the way the act of singing made me feel in my body are things I've tried so many times to describe but can never find the words.

I just can't imagine doing anything else.

So, no matter what, I must make this performance count. I don't know how, but I am going to have to figure out a way to propel it into an opportunity for a real career in Hollywood. I know there are other places I can live while being a famous singer, but in my dream, it's always been in Hollywood. Growing up in the frozen tundra, I imagine my dream life includes long days basking in the sun by the ocean, having meetings with music executives at outside cafés, and generally being surrounded by the creative energy I think Hollywood is made of.

I park my car and feel empowered, thanks to the amazing songs that just played me to my destination. I am early because I believe if you're on time, you're late. And even the thought of being close to late for this is unbearable. So, I have about twenty minutes to kill.

Isn't there a park around the corner? I think to myself. I get out of the car, straighten the dress, and think, *Yeah, Karsten and Zane were right. This dress is seriously badass.* I grab my bag and head to the park. I can get some homework done while I wait out the time.

As I turn the corner, I see a farmers' market right in front of the TV station. It continues down for about four blocks. I love farmers' markets and go searching for some honey for my daily tea-and-honey ritual. There's a fruit stand and a Mediterranean vendor. I love hummus! I spot a honey stall and head over. As the farmer tells me about the special organic lavender-infused honey he's selling, I hear sounds unlike anything I've ever heard.

I turn toward the sound, only to realize people, tents, and chairs are flying through the air. Just then, a car careens out from under a tent heading straight toward me. In a moment of clarity, I realize it's about to hit me. I take note of the people around me, and I jump out of the way. But my jump is blocked suddenly as I smack into the honey farmer's truck and fall to the ground. Immediately, the table that was on top of the sawhorses in the stall next to us comes flying at me like a bullet as the car swerves to miss me and keeps going. I am pinned to the ground. It can't be more than a second later when I hear a guttural, primal scream, only to realize it's coming from me! My leg is trapped by this table that seems to weigh a ton and feels like it's getting heavier by the second. I notice it is getting heavier because a man is at the other end, lifting it up, and, in turn, smashing it down on my leg. I try to get his attention and finally do when he realizes I'm under it. He pushes his end off to the side and reveals a woman who has been crushed underneath.

I manage to pull my leg out and hobble over to the woman. I lean over. There's a steady stream of blood coming from her head. I look up, and the person who moved the table has gone to help someone else. I sit with her for a minute, her ice-blue eyes staring at me. She's unable to speak, but I try to understand. She keeps pointing to her neck, and I realize it's because a broach she is wearing has lodged in her neck. I pull it out and am thankful no blood comes out because I am scared she's already lost too much. I ask someone walking by if they'll sit with her, and I get up to go find help.

On my way to the end of the street, I pass the honey vendor, and he signals that he's fine. It appears the only real damage to his truck is where my body slammed into it. His table is unscathed. Just then, I see a first responder. I hobble over and try to get his attention.

"I have a woman who needs help," I cry.

"Everyone needs help," he replies, seemingly in shock about what he sees.

"Yes, but this woman is bleeding from her head," I plead.

This seems to get his attention, and he snaps to work.

"Where is she?" he asks.

I lead him to her, and when I feel confident she is being taken care of, I look around to try to see if there's anyone else I can help. I scan the whole scene. It's unbelievable. Literally like something I've only seen in the movies.

My eyes land on the maroon car that only minutes earlier had taken a beautiful day and turned it into utter devastation. A group of people run past, looking for the driver. I get a chill as I hear them say, "He did it on purpose. Where is he? I heard him rev his engine before he broke through the barricade."

I survey the scene—the paramedic helping the woman with the bloody head; the man who was alive just a minute ago, lying there, dead in the middle of the street; a baby carriage tipped over; fruits and vegetables scattered all over. In and amongst the bent and ripped tents, I see an old man with glasses and grey bushy hair being pulled out of the car by a younger man. He appears to be helping the older man to sit on the curb to wait for the authorities to come and talk to him. *Is that the person? Is he the one who caused all this? Did he do it on purpose? No, I can't beli...* My thoughts are interrupted by the sound of a panicked yell.

"Steve!"

I walk over and put my hand on her shoulder and ask, "Can I help you?"

She looks at me with desperation. "I can't find my friend, Steve. He was just here."

I begin to shout his name when he comes around the corner. He had run the opposite direction when he saw the car coming down the street. They hug, and I move on.

I look down the street to where the car has stopped and see that there's a dead body lodged in the back tire, and the man who was driving is sitting, zombie-like, on the curb. I cannot fathom what I am seeing.

I look over to where I was just a few short minutes ago and notice there's a sheet over the person who was standing right next to me.

I must have just been standing there looking lost when a woman with golden blond, curly hair approaches me in the kindest way and asks, "Were you hit?"

I can't speak. I look around at the sheet-covered man who was alive and standing next to me buying groceries at a farmers' market for crying out loud, just minutes ago. I look at the man sitting on the curb. The woman who was crushed under the table is being put on a gurney, and the friends that had lost each other are now holding each other while talking to a police officer, and I decide right then and there that I'm fine.

"I was," I say through gritted teeth. "But I'm fine. I've got somewhere to be." I look down at my hands, which are clutching my bag. I don't know when I grabbed it, but I am holding onto it for dear life. And I start walking.

"Please don't go. You need to stay and be counted." The woman gestures for me to go back inside the police tape.

Be counted, I think. *Well, she's probably right. The cops need a head count, and I'm nothing if not practical.*

"Okay, but once they count me, I'm leaving." She gently puts her hand on my shoulder and leads me back into the area that the police have taped off like a crime scene.

There's a lone, white plastic chair sitting in the middle of the street that I collapse in. I look at the dress that used to be my grandma's, the dress that I am going to wear when my dreams start to come true, and notice there's blood on it. Blood! I don't know what to do. I have to perform on live television in less than an hour! How am I going to get my dress clean?

"My name is Lisa. What's yours?"

"Nif," I stutter after a minute of trying to find the words. "My name is Nif."

"That's an unusual name. Where does it come from?" she asks.

Again, I take an awkwardly long time to answer. "It's short for Jennifer."

What is happening to me? Why can't I talk? I start to panic inside when I am jarred out of my thought, hearing Lisa talking to a firefighter. I can't hear what they're saying, only whispers as I try to process everything I am seeing.

Just then, the firefighter comes over. "Alright then, let's go." As he tries to get me to go on a gurney, I see many other people still lying on the ground, so I refuse.

"Please use that for someone who can't walk. I am capable," I say as I start to hobble down the street.

Just then, it becomes like a scene in a movie. One person after another notices I am limping, and they come over to help, giving me their shoulders to lean on like a bucket brigade down the four blocks I needed to walk in order to reach triage. About halfway down, the firefighter who had tried to get me on the gurney in the first place comes by and stops the gurney next to me. "Okay, everyone who wasn't capable of making it to triage on their own has been taken there. It's your turn. Please get on the gurney."

"Okay. As long as everyone else is taken care of."

I hop on, and I gotta admit—it's nice not to be hobbling anymore.

Chapter Five

THE PARAMEDICS ROLL ME INTO TRIAGE, WHICH IS JUST an area that's been blocked off by police barricades, tape, and people, lots of people, trying to see what is going on. In the center are those of us who were injured and are waiting to be taken to one of the three area hospitals that are now overflowing with patients.

As we get wheeled in, there's a quick screening process, and we're each given a little rectangle mat to lie on while we wait. A long, perforated tag is put around one of our ankles to serve as a quick reference tool for those assessing who needs to be transported to the hospital first.

The tags that they put on our feet are long and rectangular and made so that you can rip the pieces off that don't apply to the victim. They go in this order: minor, moderate, severe, critical, deceased.

I get a very uneasy feeling as I look at this tag. I can't explain it.

I'm lying there when they put this kid next to me who is crying uncontrollably. He can't be more than eight years old, and the fear he is feeling is palpable. I reach over and try to calm him as the paramedics rush around tending to all of us. His face perks up when he hears a familiar voice call his name.

"Mama!" he yells at a woman who looks to be in her forties scanning the area for her little boy.

"My baby!" I hear her cry back.

She tries talking to him, but the noise is too loud, and he starts crying again.

"It's going to be alright." I grab his hand and squeeze. "Is that your mom?"

"Yes," he says as he looks at me with tears in his eyes.

Holding his hand seems to calm both him and his mother.

"We'll get through this together." I give him a little smile.

It feels good to hold someone's hand, and it not only helps this young boy, I think, but me as well, to stay calm and focus on getting through. I squeeze his hand as we lie there silently.

"Nif?" I don't believe my ears, so I don't react. "Nif, is that you?"

I look around and see Karen, the news reporter I was supposed to be meeting, standing there at the barricades to triage.

"Ms. Kolby, I'm so sorry I missed your show," I say naively.

She just smiles. "It's not your fault. Maybe we can have you on to talk about this."

My heart sinks, as I begin to realize that I have missed my opportunity. This was the moment my dreams were going to come true. How could I let this happen? Why didn't I just walk away, fix my hair and dress, and get on with it? What are my parents going to think? They're always saying, "The show must go on." What are the kids at school going to think? Zane and Karsten, they believe in me so much. I can't believe all the people I just let down.

"Okay, but they're making me go to the hospital."

"Maybe we can follow you there," she says as her cameraman runs up.

Just then, I feel the little boy's hand leave mine. I look over as he is being taken away, his mom following close behind. I see them embrace and feel a little bit of relief.

Suddenly, a gurney is right beside me, and I'm being hoisted upon it. It feels strange to be this out of control of things. I mean, I am capable of moving, but at this point, I just don't have the energy to fight.

The gurney pops up with a jolt, and I am being pushed away.

"What's your name?" I ask the man with the kind face who is pushing my gurney.

"Harold," he replies with a smile. "What's yours?"

"Nif."

I notice my toe tag now says *deceased.*

"Harold, am I dead?"

"Ummm, no, why would you ask that?"

"Well, my toe tag says I am, and this is all so surreal that I figured I might be having an after-death experience. But most living people can't hear the dead, so I thought I'd ask."

Just then, on a beautiful, sunny, warm autumn day, the sky opens up, and rain starts to pour down as if the heavens are crying for the loss of the day. Harold pulls a blanket over my head. I can see the people as I'm being wheeled by through a tiny sliver in the blanket. They look so concerned, and I realize that the blanket over my head mixed with my toe tag saying deceased makes them all think I'm dead.

When we reach the ambulance and Harold pulls the blanket down off of my face, I look him square in the eye and ask again, "Are you sure I'm not dead?"

He just chuckles, "You're a lively one, Nif. You are most certainly *not* dead."

All I can do is trust this man at this point, so I close my eyes and try not to cry. The sound of the sirens pierce through the air as they rush me to the hospital.

Chapter Six

THE CHAOS OF THE ACTUAL CRASH IS MATCHED BY THE chaos in the emergency room as they wheel me through the double doors.

"Bye, Harold! Thanks for everything," I say as he hands me off to the emergency room nurses and doctors.

"Nif," I hear Karen yelling through the chaos.

How the heck did she beat me here? It's so strange.

"Are you family?" I hear one of the nurses ask her.

"No, I'm a friend," I hear her say back.

Friend?! Since when did we become friends? People say the darndest things.

The nurse tells her she can't talk to me now, and I'm wheeled into a room split in half with a curtain. It turns out that the other occupant is none other than my triage buddy. I decide that once the nurses leave me on my side of the room, I'll hobble out of bed and go say hi.

"Hi," I hear from the other side of the curtain.

"Hi," I say back.

"Thank you for being so kind to my son. My name is Mary."

"Oh, I'm happy I could be there with him. My name is Nif."

She peeks her head around the corner as I sit up in bed. Her face is much more relaxed than it was at the triage area, and I breathe a little sigh of relief.

"How is he?"

"He's going to be fine. He's got a broken arm, but, all in all, he's lucky."

"Oh good," I say, not really knowing how to respond. Like, what's proper etiquette for a situation like this?

"How are you?" she asks.

"I'm fine. Just fine. Thanks for asking."

Just then her son calls her name and she excuses herself by saying thank you again.

The doctor walks in.

"Hi, Jennifer, my …"

"It's Nif," I interrupt him.

"Nif. Okay, great. Nif. My name is Dr. Max." He smiles. "Everyone is talking about how you're keeping people in good spirits."

"Nice to meet you. Yeah, I'm trying. It's a weird day." I give a nervous laugh. "When can I go home?" I feel like I can't take one more minute of this nonsense. My sense of humor is fading.

"Well, you were just in a pretty intense situation. The paramedics said you were limping when they picked you up, so I'd like to get your leg X-rayed before letting you leave. Will that be okay?" he asks as he glances at his chart.

"Fine." I try to hide my disappointment with having to stay longer. "But I'm okay. Really. This is all just silly. I'm not bleeding anywhere, and clearly, you have enough to deal with. I mean, other people were actually injured."

"Nif, I hate to break this to you, but you are one of those people. So, please let me take care of you and make sure you're really okay."

Take care of me? I shift in my seat, trying not to show how offended I am. *Ha! Good one. I am perfectly capable of taking care of myself, thank you very much.* This whole situation is truly starting to annoy me. I just want to go home and go to sleep.

I then realize that my family is expecting me to be on TV today. Oh my gosh. Do they know what's happening?

"Do you know if anyone has told my mom and dad what happened?" I say, trying to hold back the fear I feel about disappointing them.

"I'm not sure. Let me check," he says as he leaves to find someone to ask.

While he's gone, a nurse comes in and tells me Karen is asking if I'd be up for an interview. I know she's going to keep asking, and she's also my ticket out of Karlville, so I want to keep her happy. The nurse is looking at me expecting an answer so I pretend not be conflicted and say, "Sure."

The nurse leaves, and the doctor comes back.

"I'm not sure if anyone has called your family, but here's a phone you can use to call home and make sure they know to come and pick you up." He plugs the phone into a jack in the wall.

"Oh, I have my car. I don't need a ride."

"We can't release minors, so you'll need a parent to sign you out."

This whole under-eighteen thing is always messing up my life. Like, I take care of myself, my little sister, and my house when my parents are gone (which is a lot), and I'm treated like a baby in life. It's so frustrating. But whatever.

I dial home.

"Hello?" It is incredibly comforting to hear Jane's voice on the other end.

"Hey, baby sis, can I talk to Mom or Dad?" I'm working really hard to not show any of the afternoon's emotion.

"I don't know where they are. They were watching the news, waiting for you to come on, and I was in the kitchen getting a drink when they came in and said that they needed to leave. They called Peggy to sit with me and took off," she explains, sounding as annoyed as I'm feeling.

"Okay. Thanks."

"Nif, is everything okay?"

"Yeah, little lady, all is good," I say, trying to keep as calm as I can so Jane doesn't worry. "I've gotta run, though. Be good and I'll see you soon. K?"

"Okay. I will. Love you." She hangs up the phone.

While I was on the phone, my triage buddy and his family left, and I'm now alone in the room. I look down at the gown the nurse left for me to change into for X-rays. "Might as well get this over with," I mutter to myself.

I work my way to my feet. The pain in my knee seems to be getting worse. Or maybe the adrenaline is starting to wear off. Either way, it hurts like a mofo as I try to take the pantyhose and boots I'm wearing off. I notice the tiniest hole in the pantyhose from the crash. It corresponds with an even tinier scrape on my knee. I wish the size of the scrape matched the amount of pain I was feeling in that spot, but it doesn't, which just makes me feel like I'm making a bigger deal out of this than it is.

I stop for a second, looking at the tiny hole, and realize how much worse this could have been. I remember the conversation on Saturday about whether I should wear the dress to the TV station or wait until I got there to put it on. I was so nervous about being late that I stubbornly told them I was going to change at school and wear it to the station in case something happened on the drive there.

Oh god, Karsten and Zane must be so disappointed in me. They're probably sitting at home wondering why I'm not on television. All their support and belief in me, just wasted.

At that moment, the two quarters I had received as change for my honey purchase fall out of the pocket in my dress and tumble to the ground, seemingly in slow motion. I go to bend over to pick them up and lose my balance. I fall to the ground and just start sobbing. The flood of emotions is too much. The pain in my body, sorrow in my heart, guilt for letting people down, frustration for having to be in this situation at all. Just every possible emotion has piled up, and that is the tipping point. I start to wail a primal wail.

The nurse comes to get me for the X-ray, a nurse who has most likely been told that I'm the funny one, the one keeping people in good spirits. He finds me in a heap of tears on the ground.

"What happened?" he asks as he makes his way toward me.

"I just… I…" I try to find the words, but they won't come. Only tears. Lots and lots of tears. This is definitely what they mean when they talk about the floodgates opening.

The nurse just sits on the floor and holds me as I sob.

"I'm so sorry," I say between gasps, knowing I have just made his already difficult day even worse.

"It's my pleasure," he says in a calm, kind tone. "I'm so sorry for you."

I hear that and think, *No, I'm fine.* I don't want people to feel sorry for me. I pull myself together. "Thank you. Let's go to the X-ray."

I make my way to X-ray where there's a line of chairs five deep of people waiting to get in. The line is interrupted as two uniformed police officers come rushing in. They are holding a baby that can't be more than six months old in their arms, explaining to the doctor that they rushed her over in the back of their police car hoping to save her brand-new life. I overhear them say her mom is in surgery because she cushioned the blow of the car when it hit them.

I try not to lose it again.

"Were you in the crash?" the man in the chair next to me asks, thankfully startling me out of what would definitely be a thought spiral.

"Excuse me?"

"Were you in this crash that everyone is talking about?" he asks again with concern on his face.

"Yes. You weren't?" I say, assuming that's the only reason anyone would be in the hospital, forgetting that the world doesn't stop just because something like this happens.

"No. I'm here because I have gangrene in my thumb," he responds, showing me something I can't unsee.

"Oh gosh," I blurt out, feeling immediately embarrassed by my inability to be polite. It's just that his thumb looks like a moldy piece of meat that's been forgotten about in the back of the refrigerator, and I don't really know how to respond, so I look him straight in the eyes, trying not to look down. "That looks painful. Are you alright?"

"I might lose my thumb," he states with little emotion, which I find odd.

I'm startled away from focusing on the disgusting pussy mess that is this man's thumb, by the sound of the X-ray light going on across the hall in front of me. The doctor throws up the X-ray of the little baby, and I can see all the wires coming out of her chest.

I put my head in my hands and just sob quietly, feeling grateful for all the chaos around me as I hope it will hide my emotion from everyone.

"Nif! Oh thank god!" I hear my mom yell from down the hall. She generally has no awareness of how loud she is, and right now is no exception. I look up to see her and my dad running toward me. I wipe my eyes quickly and try to smile, wincing from the pain in my knee as I try to stand. We lock eyes, and the embarrassment of everyone looking at us disappears as I get the hug I have desperately needed all day.

"Mom, Dad!" I bury my head in their chests as they hug me so tight I can barely breathe.

"I'm okay. I'm okay," I try to reassure them.

"What's going on?" Dad asks, grabbing my shoulders in a sort of desperate-to-understand manner.

"I have to get an X-ray of my knee," I explain, trying to keep a stiff upper lip. "But I'm sure it's nothing."

As I get wheeled to the X-ray room, I look back to see my mom and dad embracing each other. Relief and worry can be seen on both their faces.

After the X-ray, they wheel me by the machine where the baby's X-ray is still hanging. It's dark now, but that image is etched in my mind along with the image of the lady with the bleeding head, the man who was standing next to me, alive, and then lying under a sheet, dead, and so many more images that I wish I could erase. I realize I haven't asked about the woman with the bleeding head, and I turn around and ask the nurse pushing my wheelchair if she knows anything.

"I'm afraid we can't give out that information."

"I understand," I say back, my voice wobbly with emotion. "I just helped her get an ambulance, and I thought she might die and am wondering," I start to babble. The words just aren't coming out right.

The nurse nods. "Let me see what I can do."

"Thank you." I mean it deeply.

Back in my room, my parents are waiting for me. We're still alone, and it's a bit strange. My parents don't know what to say, I can't find the words, and no one knows what to do. So, my dad paces and my mom keeps getting up to see if anyone is coming in the hallway.

The doctor finally comes in and explains that nothing is broken, but I'm going to have to be on crutches for a few days, and then he suggests going to see some specialists. He wishes me luck and sends us on our way.

The nurse who was wheeling me from X-ray comes back and reminds me that Karen is waiting to interview me. *Oh man, I totally forgot.*

"And I checked on the woman you asked about, and she is going to be just fine. It wasn't a head injury.

It was her ear. Her family is with her, and she's going home soon."

"Oh my gosh. Thank you. Thank you. Thank you." Tears of relief pour from my eyes.

My parents just look at me, concerned. They've never seen me cry like that before, and I feel silly doing it now, but I can't help it. It's like my whole body is so full of energy that the tears are its way of releasing it. My shoulders sink, and I realize I'm too tired to care.

Just as we're getting ready to leave, Karen spots us.

"Nif, are you ready for that interview?" she asks as if she's a starving hyena and I'm an injured rabbit.

My parents step in and try to postpone, but I am still keenly aware that this woman may possess my ticket out of Karlville, and I want to get out of there now more than ever.

"It's okay, guys. I'll be fine," I declare with as reassuring a voice as I can muster. "Let's do it."

After Karen and her cameraman take me to the "perfect" spot in the hospital, we do a 10-minute interview about the day's events, and then I get ready to leave the hospital.

"What about my car?" I ask, starting to panic. I don't think I can drive, but know I might need to because I can't just leave my car. I can hear the unintentional hysteria resonating in my voice.

My dad puts his hand on my shoulder and calmly says, "It's okay. I'll drive your car. Where are your keys?"

Relieved, I open up my backpack to pull out the keys. They're all sticky. Apparently, my backpack had actually gotten crushed somehow, and the honey I had bought had leaked all over everything. I start to cry as I pull out my homework, notebooks, keys, everything. It's all ruined.

Ugh, these darn tears. Where the flip are they coming from, I think, super annoyed that I so easily cry. I don't feel like myself.

I apologize to my dad and hand him my keys. "Wait. I have wet wipes. I can clean them with those." I frantically search through my bag.

Finding them completely covered in honey, I give up and cry some more. Which leads to me being more frustrated, which leads to more crying.

"Nif, your dad can take care of it. Just give him your bag and we'll head home."

I hesitantly hand over the bag. It feels strange not to be holding onto it. But I feel relief when I finally pass through the automatic doors of the hospital.

We've nearly made it to the car when Karen spots us and comes running up. "Oh, I almost forgot to ask—do you want to do the show tomorrow since you weren't able to do it today?"

I am too stunned to respond, and also I have no idea what to say. I mean, I am leaning on my crutches, my clothes are dirty, I have tear stains all over my face, and I can't imagine I look like I can pull myself together enough to sing.

Keep it together. Keep it together. I can't find the words.

My mom, who is usually really good at letting me make decisions for myself, looks at me for the first time, and, in a way that only a mother can do, reads my mind. She steps in and answers for me, "I don't think tomorrow is going to work, but let me get her home, and we'll call you to reschedule."

"Oh, okay." Karen sounds completely shocked. "But we'd like Nif to perform even if it's at half her normal capacity. She's just so talented."

My mom nods to let Karen know she heard her, gives her a half smile, puts her hands gently on my shoulders, and leads me to the car.

Karen's tone rings in my ear the entire ride home. *How could she be surprised that I couldn't perform tomorrow? I mean, did she really expect it? Is this really the thing that kills my dreams? Will she tell everyone in the world that I'm not good enough to be a pro because I couldn't pull myself up by my bootstraps and just get on with it? Why can't I be stronger?*

Chapter Seven

We walk in the door, and I'm almost knocked over by the leaping hugs coming at me from Karsten and Zane.

"We saw you on the news!" Karsten practically yells.

"Oh, gosh, sorry," Zane says when she realizes I'm on crutches. She starts to clear a path through the piles of laundry, and they begin to fuss over me, which makes me feel super awkward.

"I'm fine. Just let me sit down."

"Of course. Of course." Zane reacts in her most Zen tone of voice.

"Tell us everything." Karsten grabs my hand, pulling me toward the living room. His normal way of being is really irking me right now. It's not like I was just in a little fender-bender. I saw three people die and so many more things that I'll never be able to get out of my head. How can he ask me to relive that?

In that moment, I can feel my brain just snap off. It's the weirdest feeling. I can see my friends and family, I can feel Jane sitting in my lap hugging me, and I can hear the buzzing around me, but I have no idea what anyone is saying. It's like my head is in the middle of a clear, see-through beehive. I look at Karsten, so he knows I hear him, but that's all I can do. I can't form thoughts or words. Everything is just… snapped off.

Karsten sees this and just sits on the couch and holds my hand. I can tell he's concerned, but I can't find a way to do… well… anything. Nothing but sit.

My mom says something, but I don't really comprehend, and suddenly, I'm being given my crutches, and we're walking toward my bedroom. I abruptly go into the bathroom and mindlessly make my way into the shower. The water feels so nice on my skin, and I begin to sob. The water hides the tears, and I let go even more. My whole body shakes with each sob as the water pours over my face. I hope the shower will wash every single thing I saw and experienced today right down the drain.

I peel back the shower curtain to see that someone put a clean pair of pajamas on the counter. I feel so grateful as the soft fabric brushes my skin. Pajamas are one of the greatest pleasures in life, in my opinion. I just love them so much. As I feel gratitude for the pajamas, a flash of the man who was standing next to me comes rushing into my head. *Did he like pajamas?* I think. *Does his wife? Did he even have a wife? Oh gosh, what if he had kids? Did they take those cute family pictures in matching pajamas at the holidays? If not, did he plan to? He's never going to have that opportunity.* The thoughts start racing, and tears start coming, and my mom comes through the door right as I fall to the ground. She holds me tight, and I breathe in her perfume as I cry.

They don't come to the bathroom in that moment, but I can feel that my friends and Jane are on the other side of that wall probably thinking, *What the hell is going on?* My mom walks me to my room without the dumb crutches, and I limp to my bed and lie down. Once I settle in, I look up, and everyone is there hovering over me like those weird shots from a baby's point of view that they do in movies.

"Guys! I'm fine. Really." I let out a little laugh. "I'm not dead. Quit treating this like it's a funeral. I feel like I'm in a coffin, and you all are staring at me. Knock it off."

My analogy of the coffin seems to have made everyone feel a little better, and they all let out a collective sigh-giggle.

My dad walks into my room. "I've cleaned your keys, washed your car, put gas in the tank, and cleaned your backpack the best I could."

"Thanks, Dad," I say with a smile, "I'm really tired. I'm going to try and get some sleep, if that's alright?"

Everyone starts to get up with a chorus of, "Of course. Sure. Okay," as they leave.

"We're really happy you're alive, Nif." Zane gives me a hug on her way out.

Karsten squeezes my hand in solidarity.

"I love you two."

My body just gives way to exhaustion, and sleep takes over.

A few hours later, I jolt up in bed, woken by my own screams. Tears stream down my face. My parents charge through my door.

"What's wrong?" my dad asks in as calm a voice as he can muster, but I can see the worry in his eyes.

I can't talk. I can barely breathe as I try to catch my breath and stop the tears.

"I don't know. I just woke up like this."

They hold me as my body tries to let out whatever I had just dreamed. The terror I am feeling must be a small bit of what I was feeling when I was asleep because my body is so stiff that it takes a conscious effort to relax it, and as each muscle relaxes, it's like I'm massaging out a Charlie horse. The pain and tightness are intense enough to cause even more tears, but, at this point, I can't tell what's causing the crying. I just know I hate it, and it won't stop.

My mom comes in with some sleeping medicine. I push it away. "I can't take that. It's already 2 a.m. What if I sleep through my alarm and I'm late for school?"

"Are you serious?" my mom asks. "Baby, you are not going to school tomorrow," she says in her sternest voice, which just makes me want to argue even more.

"Yes. I am. I have a private singing lesson with Mrs. M and a history test that I've been studying for for two weeks. I *have* to go."

"These are all things that can be made up. It's just one day. You can go back to school on Wednesday." The way she is talking makes me know there is no more debating the issue.

I'm too tired to argue at this point, and the medication is taking over. I fall asleep. It's not very good sleep, but at least I don't wake the whole house up again.

I wake up at 7 a.m. to the sound of my mom on the phone. "No, Mrs. Clark, Nif won't be coming in today. Yes, Mrs. Clark, she's fine. No, Mrs. Clark, I don't know if the man did it intentionally. Okay, Mrs. Clark, I have to go now. Okay, thank you. Yup. Okay, bye."

She hangs up the phone, and I hear her mumble to herself, "Ugh, if this town spent as much time doing things that mattered as they do gossiping… I swear."

She peeks her head into my room and sees that I'm awake. "Nif, hey honey, how are you?"

"I'm fine. Just going to take a day to reset. Then back to normal so those people won't be asking stupid questions anymore. Like, why do they even care? It's not that big a deal."

My mom doesn't respond, which is weird, but it's been a long night, so I chalk it up to her being tired.

"I'm glad you're going to rest. And I mean rest. I don't want you doing anything but watching cheesy movies today."

Dad pokes his head into the room right behind her. "Good morning. Your mom and I have a meeting with a new band that's interested in recording in our studio, so we're going to give them a tour and then take them out to lunch. But we'll be sure to keep them out of this area of the house so you get some rest."

"Nif!" Jane yells as she does a running leap through my bedroom door and onto my bed, hitting my knee in a way that sort of knocks the wind out of me.

"Careful." Mom gives Jane a look that only a mom can give. "Nif hurt her knee, remember?"

"Oh, right. Sorry." Jane hesitantly climbs back down off my bed.

I grab her and say, "The damage is already done, my lil sis," as I pull her in for a hug.

"Okay, get your stuff, Jane. I'll drop you off at school since Nif isn't going to be able to walk with you today." Dad winks at me, and I smile back.

They leave, and Mom goes down to the studio to prep for the tour. I make my way to the couch and turn on the TV to settle in for the day.

One day of rest and relaxation ought to do it, I think to myself. *If I truly take the day to rest, I should be at 100 percent tomorrow, and this whole mumbo jumbo will be behind me.*

Chapter Eight

"Okay, you're going to be fine. It's gonna be alllll good. Don't worry," I say sternly to my reflection as I swipe away the steam on the bathroom mirror, trying to calm myself down as I get ready to be bombarded with dumb questions back at school. Turns out this thing is a bigger deal than I thought, and *everyone* is talking about it. Zane and Karsten came over last night and told me all about how everyone is asking if the man did it on purpose, if I will be suing, and if I am okay (that last one definitely seems like an afterthought for these gossip vultures).

I tug at my shirt, smile at myself, and nod. *Okay, I'm ready.* I turn to leave the bathroom only to see the dreaded crutches. *Ugh, these dumb things. So annoying.* I grab them anyway, take a deep breath, and make my way to the driveway. Since I am on crutches, Dad is driving Jane to school again so I don't have to worry about her accidentally tripping me. I'm grateful for that. He's also dropping me off since I can't drive.

I get to the car and manage to get myself and my crutches in. Dad and Jane can both see how annoyed I am, so they don't say anything as we drive the five blocks to the high school. I get out of the car, wave, grab my crutches, and head into school.

I walk through the doors, and everyone, and I mean *everyone,* is staring at me. To make matters worse, the crutches make this loud creaking sound with every step I make. I try to keep a smile on my face. I think to myself, *Wow, is this what it feels like to be famous?* Celebrities are always talking about how it feels like you can't do anything without someone watching you, the fishbowl effect. And if this *is* what it feels like, it has me rethinking my dream of being famous.

Remember, aggressive optimism, I think to myself. I've been working on it since the crash. It isn't working well, but I feel like it's something to hold on to, so I'm trying.

I've been told to go to the office first since the school is still in the middle of installing an elevator.

"Hi, Mrs. Clark." Our school admin sits behind the counter of the front office like a jackal waiting to pounce on its prey as I walk into the principal's office. "Principal Morgan wanted to see me before class."

"Oh, yes, dear. Come in, come in. How are you? Take a seat. Can I get you anything?" she says as if I'm the Queen of England.

"I'm fine. Thank you."

I get halfway to a sitting position when Principal Morgan opens the door to let me in. *Don't they know how much extra work it is to use these stupid things,* I think to myself as I put on a fake smile and start toward the office.

"Nif, I'm so sorry you had to go through all of that."

"It's okay. I'd like to just get back to normal as quickly as possible. I understand you wanted to have this meeting so we could discuss how I can get to my classes since the elevator isn't installed yet."

I could tell that wasn't the *real* reason Principal Morgan wanted to have this meeting. She just wanted to see if she could get more info for the gossip mill. Ugh. I hate this town.

I continue before she can say anything. "I was thinking about it, and, honestly, I don't think there will be an issue. My locker is on the second floor, and all my classes are as well. The only reason I would need to change floors during the day is to go to lunch, but I brought my own, so I should be fine. I'll just make my way slowly up to the second floor in the morning and stay up there until the end of the day. Should be fine." I muster up as much pep as I can.

"Well, okay, then," Principal Morgan says, flustered. "Seems like you've got it all planned out."

"I do. Thanks," I reply back in a way that has her knowing I'm ready to leave.

"Alright, if you need anything, anything at all, even just to talk, please don't hesitate to come to my office."

"Okay, thanks." That definitely won't happen. Principal Morgan and Mrs. Clark are a center point for the gossip mill in Karlville, and they've been nothing but sneaky, backstabbing monsters to my family ever since we moved here.

I politely say goodbye to everyone in the office, intent on getting to my locker as quickly as possible. Slowly maneuvering between the horde, getting ready for first period, I see Zane and Karsten are waiting for me at the base of the stairs.

"Oh, man, am I happy to see the two of you." They have both come in a little early to help me.

Zane grabs my books, Karsten grabs my crutches, I grab the handrail, and we begin to go up the stairs, but our plans are foiled by the onslaught of questions at each and every step.

We finally make it to the first landing, where we regroup in the corner.

"This isn't working. It's taken like ten minutes just to get here, and we have a whole other flight to get up." I lift my shoulders, stand up straight, and, in my most matter-of-fact, productive, "let's get this done sort of way," begin to shout out orders.

I can tell by Zane and Karsten's reaction that they missed this part of my personality even though it was only for a day. I think they thought it was gone forever. No way. I'm not going to let this stop me from accomplishing my goals.

"Okay, Zane, you carry both my bag and my crutches."

"Check," she replies with an abrupt head nod for effect.

"Karsten, I need you on crowd control. You need to make a hole. 'No autographs' style. Copy?"

"Copy that," he replies as he puts himself into position.

"Okay, let's go," I say in my most militant voice.

We make it to the top of the stairs and all the way down the hall to my locker just as the first bell rings. Luckily, I have either Karsten or Zane in all my classes except choir. But the choir room is like five feet from my locker, so I'm good to go.

I make it through my first two classes. My third class is choir, and I get there early since it's so close to my locker. A group of my fellow singers come over to check in with me. They are being so nice, and I feel super supported. Jessa and her cronies walk in right as the second bell rings and see all the other students leave my area. I can feel her disapproval from across the room.

"Everyone find their seats." Mrs. M claps her hands above her head to make sure we're paying attention as she walks over to the piano. "Let's start with our warmups." She hits the keys in the chord of C. "Okay, then… many mumbling mince…" We all start to sing.

The vibration of the voices coming together along with the act of singing is just what the doctor ordered, and I feel "normal" for the first time in days. The class ends, and I am on a high as I head to the bathroom before lunch. It takes me twice as long as everyone else to get anywhere with these crutches, so when I finally get there, Jessa is already in there, primping in the mirror.

"Well, well, if it isn't Little Miss Faaamoousss." Jessa draws out the word *famous* as if she's the queen of the South. Gosh I hate her stupid way of talking.

As Jane would say, "It's so lame."

"Hi, Jessa," I say, not trying at all to hide my annoyance with her.

"So, Nif, how does it feel to finally get all that fame and popularity you dreamed of? But to know that you couldn't get it because of your actual talent? I guess it doesn't really matter though, right? Fame is fame, after all." Her voice drips with sarcasm and bile.

Remember, Jessa and I were friends before we weren't, so she knows how much these words hurt. I talked to her about my dreams and how important it was to me to become successful and famous through the work and not just luck into fame because of talent because, according to my parents, work ethic is just as important as talent.

In true Jessa style, she holds her gaze until she knows she has hit a nerve and then spins around on her heel, leaving me there to sit with what she said. This is all stuff I'm used to. But, for some reason, in this moment, it's all too much, and I start to not only feel the tears, but have a feeling in my chest that is brand-new.

It starts slowly, but before I know it, I can't breathe and start gasping for air. My crutches fall to the ground first, and then I fall. I think I might die, and it feels like I'm suffocating from a giant elephant standing on my chest. I start to hyperventilate.

It must be loud because Zane and Karsten come rushing into the bathroom. I can barely hear Zane tell Karsten to get the school nurse right before I pass out.

As I come to, my head in Zane's lap, I see the bathroom is blocked like an entrance to the most exclusive club. The nurse looks horrified. Not the most calming thing to wake up to, by the way.

I slowly get up and shake it off.

"What happened?" Zane asks while the nurse is checking my pulse with her hand on my wrist.

"I don't know. One minute, you-know-who was in here picking on me, per usual. And, the next minute, I couldn't breathe, and then I must have passed out."

The nurse explains that she thinks I had a panic attack and that I should go see my doctor as soon as possible. She leaves, saying she's going to call my parents to come and pick me up.

I just looked at Zane and ask, "What's a panic attack?" and start to cry. "This whole ordeal is exhausting and, quite frankly, annoying. Now I have to go home… *again*?"

Zane looks at me with concern. "We're coming with you."

"Yeeessss! Playing hooky sounds perfect," Karsten replies, snapping his fingers in excitement.

I don't argue because I know the two of them are always looking for reasons to get out of school. They aren't like me. They aren't fighting to get out. Their families founded this town, so they can pretty much get away with anything. No one messes with them, and they are both super content to live here forever.

Karsten leaves his post at the door with his arms held wide, saying, "Group huuuugggs."

We all laugh and hug. Karsten hands me my crutches just as Mrs. M comes flying through the doors. She looks around frantically. We lock eyes for a brief second, but I quickly look away. I can't handle the look of concern in her eyes. I can't handle that I'm doing that to someone I care for so much. She hadn't been there for the whole scene, and she's now looking to me for an explanation.

I just don't have the energy, and Zane and Karsten can sense it, so they guide me out the door as I avert my eyes and quietly mumble a hello as we walk past her.

"Nif, are you okay?" she asks, following us out of the bathroom.

"I'm fine, Mrs. M. I'll see you tomorrow." I stumble past her, trying to get out of there as quickly as I can.

Two weeks later, I throw open the doors of the choir room, crutches-free, I might add. After the panic attack, my parents wanted me to take it easy, so they made me stay home. I protested at first, but then gave in because, honestly, I didn't want to deal with the whispers and really didn't want to have another panic attack. I feel like this whole thing is just adding fuel to the fire of how awfully this town feels they can treat my family. But I'm back now, and things seem to have died down a bit.

I feel super embarrassed for having just left Mrs. M in the lurch, but I try to cover it up with a chipper, "Hey, Mrs. M! You wanted to see me?"

"Yes, I wanted to check in with you and make sure you're okay."

"Oh, I'm fine." I'm feeling energized. I mean, why shouldn't I? I slept a whole four hours last night. It's the most sleep I've gotten since the crash. Not one nightmare. It might have something to do with the sleeping pill my mom gave me, but I'm not going to question it. Just enjoy it. "I saw a doctor last week who diagnosed me with post-traumatic stress disorder. But, when she explained what it was, I told her that I couldn't possibly have *that*. That's something soldiers get, and I'm not a soldier, so clearly she's wrong. She told me I needed to see a psychologist anyway, so my mom made me an appointment for tomorrow. But I am fine. No need to worry, Mrs. M. Sorry if I caused a ruckus."

Mrs. M chuckles. "Only you would be worried about everyone else at a time like this. I want you to know that you can always come to me with anything."

"Thanks, Mrs. M." But, deep down, I know I won't because I don't want her to think I can't handle stress. Being a famous singer is really stressful, and I need to suck this up and move on.

"Mrs. M, I really do better when I have something to focus on. Before all this craziness, you had mentioned you were having auditions for the holiday concert solos. Did I miss them?"

"You did, dear. But, in anticipation of your return, I told everyone that no decision would be made until you got your chance to audition as well. So, do you have a piece prepared?"

"No." *Crap!* In all the hubbamaroll, I forgot to *actually* prepare. *No worries*, I tell myself. *You got this. Just ask her for some sheet music and get to it.*

"Do you have some sheet music you'd like to hear me sing?" I ask, trying to keep calm. I really don't want to let Mrs. M down, and I know how much she needs for us to be prepared to audition. It's one of the main parts of being a professional. I can't believe I've dropped the ball so much.

"Try this one." She hands me some red-and-green-colored sheet music that has clearly been around since the music department started at the school.

I take the tattered paper from her hands and put it on the music stand in front of me. I recognize the song title but don't know the lyrics well enough to feel confident.

I fake it, though. "Oh, this song. I *love* this song."

"Great!" Mrs. M pounds out the intro on the piano with ease and precision.

I look down at the paper and begin to sing the first line when something happens in my brain. It literally feels like a record is skipping. I look at the paper and can see the words, but don't really know what I'm seeing. Skip, skip, skip is what it feels like my brain is doing. *Are words coming out of my mouth?* I look up and see Mrs. M looking at me, confused.

She stops playing. "Okay, Nif, let's try that again."

I sing the first line and then—skip, skip, skip—it starts to happen again. What the heck is my brain doing? Why can't I read the words? I have no idea what is going on. This feeling of tingling I now know to identify as panic starts to creep into my stomach, then to my throat, and before I know it, I'm down on the ground again, hyperventilating. Mrs. M comes down to the ground and holds my head. I can see her and the look of terror on her face, but I can't get to her through the fog that has now engulfed me as I see the car from that day come racing towards me. All I want to do is let her know I'm okay, but I can't. It's like my body isn't my own, and before I know it, I pass out in her arms.

When I come to, the nurse is there again, but, this time, it's just the three of us. I am grateful for that.

"Oh gosh," I say, feeling how hot my face is from embarrassment "I'm so sorry."

"It's okay. Are you okay?" Mrs. M asks.

"Her pulse is back to normal." The nurse talks to Mrs. M as if I'm not even there.

What the heck is happening, I think angrily. I just want to yell and scream at my own body and brain. *Get it together, Nif. For crying out loud. What the? Ugh.* I have to calm myself down, or the tears will definitely come.

I make my way to my feet feeling a little dizzy. "I'm fine. I'm so sorry, again." I head out the door, grateful not to have those stupid crutches so my exit can be quick.

I walk into the hallway, determined to go about my business as if everything is the same as it was before. That's possible, right? Like, people are in horrible events all the time, and they're fine afterward. This isn't any different. That's it. I'm done with this. I'm moving on.

Chapter Nine

WALKING AS QUICKLY AS I CAN, I HEAD STRAIGHT TO my room, throw my bag on my bed, and shut my door, careful to be quiet about it so I don't draw attention to myself. The last thing I need is to be disturbed by Jane with questions of whether or not I'm okay. I'm fine, damnit!

Right, right, you're fine. You're fine. You've just gotta figure this out. Aggressive optimism, right? I'm trying to remind myself to be positive, but remembering how my brain worked just a few weeks ago makes me even more frustrated. Why is it so flipping hard to focus?

Calm down. Just calm down, I tell myself, taking deep breaths. *Just breathe.* The more upset I get, the more likely I am to have another panic attack, and those suckers hurt. I'm so tired of hyperventilating. My throat is constantly raw from it, and my lungs feel like they're on fire. *You can be calm. It's going to be okay.*

The replay of today's events in the choir room has been haunting me all day. But, still energized from my four hours of sleep, I'm more determined than ever to put this crap behind me and figure out how to get a solo in the holiday show. Think. Think. Think.

I know! I've done it before, I've never had to read sheet music in order to sing my favorite pop songs. I'll just get a copy of the song I'm going to use to audition and memorize it like I would a pop song. Duh. I can't believe I haven't thought of this before. Now, which song do I want to learn?

One of the benefits of having parents that own their own recording studio is the massive song library they have. "To the basement!" I announce, raising my hand in the air, pretending to lead the imaginary troops.

Grateful my parents are out playing a gig, I head down to their studio in the basement. It's the nicest part of our house. Honestly, it actually looks like a completely different building. Our upstairs in a cozy, little, small-town house with comfortable, lived-in furniture and family pictures on the walls. The basement, on the other hand, is full of wood panels, instruments, mixing boards, mid-century modern furniture, and a massive wall of computer equipment. Which is where I am currently scouring the sound library for the perfect song. I'm just hoping Mrs. M will give me another chance so I can blow her away with my perfect rendition of… what? Yeah, good question. Rendition of what?

What the heck am I going to sing? Looking at the library of hundreds of songs, I fight back feelings of overwhelm. It's okay. Just think… what kind of song do you think Mrs. M would like to hear? It's gotta be upbeat, right? Or is she looking for more of a classic? Ugh, quit trying to figure out what she might like and remember what she always says. "If you sing a song you love to sing, the audience will love it too." Okay, Mrs. M… I want to sing… "Silent Night." Perfect! I already know all the words, so no worries there, and Mom and Dad have a kind of jazzy version right here.

I grab the music track, plug it into my player, and push play. The familiar sound fills my skin with the feeling of a warm fireplace on a cold winter's night, and I know I've found the perfect song. I hop in the recording booth since it's soundproof, so I won't have to talk to Jane about what I'm doing, and begin to sing. If the pores in my body could make a sound, they would be saying aaahhhh. I feel the calmest I've felt since the crash.

Three hours later, I head upstairs with a pep in my step and a smile on my face. I make myself a cup of tea. As I reach for the honey, my body shudders as the memory of smashed honey on the ground tries to creep its way in. Not today. I push that memory aside by remembering what just happened downstairs. A small grin crosses my face as I've successfully achieved my goal of not remembering. That smirk grows into an actual smile as I walk to my room, sipping my tea while I get ready for bed.

Chapter Ten

"I SAW THREE PEOPLE DIE THAT DAY," I BLUBBER ALMOST inaudibly through the snot-filled sobs as I recount the day's events in great detail per instructions. It took a good fifteen minutes of the therapist coaxing me to finally open up. And this is why. This, right here. The blubbering mess you see before you. This is why I don't want to ever talk about that flipping day again. I can't explain to you how much I hate crying. I hate feeling like a victim. It wasn't even that bad. Seriously, I've said it time and time again, there are people experiencing far worse things than me. But she asked, and so here I am, baring my soul, using her entire box of tissue, describing things I didn't think were possible for a person to see in real life.

An alarm sounds with the soft chimes used in Buddhist meditation to signify the end of a session. I blow my nose—ugh, disgusting! I look up, blinking, until the figure in front of me becomes the shape of a person instead of the blob she's been for the last half an hour when I realize she's sleeping. SLEEPING! I frantically try to think of what to do. Do I wake her up? Do I just sit there and wait? Clearly, she must have heard the chime. *Apparently not, Nif. Duh, she's clearly sleeping.* Is she okay? I mean, I can't imagine falling asleep during that story. *Clearly, you were right! It isn't that big of a deal. I mean, you can't even keep your therapist interested, and they're PAID to be interested.*

Oh good, movement, I think as she begins to jostle awake when the louder buzzer comes through the speaker on the wall, signifying her next patient is waiting in the waiting area. "Oh," she mumbles, clearly embarrassed. "Okay, that's all for today. We'll see you next week." She awkwardly gets to her feet like Bambi when he was first born.

"Okay." I gather my things as quickly as possible, still trying not to make her feel bad.

The cool breeze on my face feels incredible after all the crying I just did. I make my way the two blocks to my car. *Maybe she didn't sleep last night. I mean, if anyone knows how that is, it's you, Nif. Cut her some slack. But this clearly means I don't need therapy, right? I mean, if it was as bad as everyone is saying, the professional in the room wouldn't have fallen asleep. Yes, that's right. If it was something I needed help with, that whole situation would have been different. Okay, you're fine.*

Wee-woo, wee-woo, wee-woo. An ambulance rushes past as I feel my skirt blow up in a gust, the sound pierces my body, and I am suddenly on the ground, back at the crash, the maroon car screaming toward me as I scream the primal scream that has now become so familiar to me. No one on the quiet street seems to have noticed as I am coming out of this flashback alone on the sidewalk. Embarrassed, I cross my legs and move closer to the grass to try and make it look like I'm sitting there on purpose. I'm unable to fight back the sobs that my body so clearly needs to get out as I bend forward, putting my head as close to my knees as I can. I'm grateful I'm alone because that one scared even me.

Exhausted, I lift myself to my feet and walk the rest of the way to my car, where I sit for a minute and cry some more. *This can't be my life forever. It just can't. I mean, what's the point? Why did I survive only to have this be my life? I wish the car would have… Nope. Nope. Nope. Nif, stop feeling sorry for yourself. Remember, it's not that bad. I mean, the therapist fell asleep. That's a clear sign that what you went through isn't that big of a deal.*

Taking a deep breath, I turn the key and set off for home with determination. Tomorrow is a new day, and all will be better after a good night's sleep.

Chapter Eleven

Errrrrrrr—the stretch feels so good as each of my muscles soak in a little more oxygen. I am enjoying the yoga routine I got from Zane's Nana very much. I sit up and face the big window in my bedroom and can feel the warm sun on my face as a smile appears out of nowhere. *Alright, today's the day, Nif. Today's the day you move on with your life. That's it. No more of this wallowing.*

Jane gently knocks on my door, which I appreciate because my body is not responding to sudden… well, anything… very well lately. She tentatively opens the door and then pushes it wide open when she sees me smiling. "Oh good, you're awake. The 'rents," (another Jane-ism), "need you to take me to school." Normally, I would argue since school is only a few blocks away, but today, I'm feeling good.

So, I say, still smiling, "No problem." Jane looks at me suspiciously, clearly expecting a fight, but then shrugs and backs out of the room, closing the door even more gently than when she first came in.

"It's gonna be a good day," I repeat over and over to my reflection as I get ready for school.

I must have put on the right outfit because everyone wants to talk to me as I make my way into school and to my locker, where Karsten and Zane are waiting to hear all about my therapy session.

"Well, don't leave us in suspense." Zane leans against the locker to block anyone else from hearing.

"Yeah, what the hell, Nif? You didn't even call last night." I hear that Karsten flair as he walks up behind us and blocks the other side from being able to hear. "You know you're the first to officially go to therapy. It's like you're getting a jump start on your life in Hollywood already, and you're holding out on what it's really like. Spill."

"Honestly, it wasn't a big deal." I so badly want to tell them about my therapist falling asleep, but not wanting to get into it. "I just told her what happened, and she basically was, like, no big deal."

"Did she say *that*?" Zane asks in disbelief.

"Well, not exactly, but it was implied by her behavior."

"Behavior?" Karsten fishes for more details.

"Oop, the bell, gotta go." I scurry off to my first class.

"This conversation isn't over, young lady!" Karsten yells after me.

I know, I think to myself, super annoyed. But I'm grateful to have the time to think about what to say or, more importantly, how not to say anything.

I take a seat in my first-period class and wait for the TV to come on. It's Wednesday, and that's the day our weekly news show airs. Both Zane and Karsten work on it. Zane is a writer, and Karsten does hair, makeup, and wardrobe. I've never told anyone, but I long to be one of the anchors in front of the camera. However, that coveted spot is reserved for only the prettiest and most popular kids in our class. I am not one of them, so I just watch, wishing I was as cool as them.

"Good morning, Karlville High!" comes out of the TV speaker. "It is with a heavy heart that I share that I'm moving next week and will no longer be able to report on the happenings in our great school each week." Maggie, the most popular girl in our school, is on the school news, fighting back fake, pageant tears. A collective gasp occurs in the room.

That means there's a spot open on the show, I think to myself with hope. *Don't be stupid, Nif. You are absolutely not popular or pretty enough to even be considered. Why would you even think that you could get to be on the show? Ugh, you're the worst at getting your hopes up. Stop it!*

Frantically doodling in my notebook, I try to ignore the TV. I mean, I am definitely more popular now than I was before the crash. Maybe it is possible.

Oh great! You should absolutely use the most horrible day in so many people's lives to gain popularity and make your own dreams come true. God, what kind of monster are you? I scream-think. *You're right. You're right. Those are horrible thoughts. If they even ask you to fill the spot, you have to turn them down because they would only be asking because of what you went through, not because you're actually who they want to fill the job. It's like Jessa keeps saying. I couldn't get popular through my own merit, only because of this stupid thing that happened to me. Ugh, I hate it when she's right.*

I put the thought out of my head as I go about my day.

"Nif, come sit with us," I hear someone yell as I walk into the cafeteria. I look over to see Maggie slide to make room for me among all the most popular kids at school.

Did I hear her right? Did she really say *my* name? I look around me to make sure she's not talking to someone behind me. No. No one is there. I begin to walk over, hesitantly, until I hear her say, "Nif, sit right here," as she pats the seat next to her. "Nif, what an unusual name." I search her tone for mockery, anticipating my exit. Maggie has never ever in the history of my time at Karlville High given me the time of day. Why is she asking me about my name now?

But she seems genuinely curious, so I explain, "Oh, it's short for Jennifer. You know, like, Jen-nif-er. My grandma has called me Nif since I was born." I try to make it sound cooler than it is.

"Oh, that's cool. I love that your grandma gave you such a neat nickname." She smiles that big perfect smile. *She's really nice*, I think to myself, remembering all the awful things Zane and Karsten have said about her in the past. I try to remember that and not get too friendly or let my guard down too much. But I must admit I am enjoying talking with her. And everyone sitting at the *popular* table seems so nice, maybe Karsten and Zane are wrong about the popular kids.

"Oh, hey, sorry we couldn't make it to lunch today." Zane shuffles up behind me. Her seeming inability to lift her feet entirely off the ground when she walks used to be endearing to me, but lately the noise is jarring, and I feel agitated when we walk together.

Ugh, stop feeling so annoyed. She's one of your best friends! You love her! I think to myself. It's true; I do.

I never thought I would have as good a friend as her, so I'm annoyed that I'm annoyed.

"All good," I say, trying to hide my annoyance. "Maggie actually invited me to sit at her table. We had a really great time."

"You *did?*" Zane looks at me with complete shock as Karsten dramatically slow runs to catch up.

"What's up?" he asks, noticing the look on Zane's face.

"Your girl had lunch with Maggie and crew today," Zane tells Karsten in her most exasperated—which really isn't exasperated at all because she's essentially a Buddha—tone.

"Gasp! What? Are you serious? That's like going to the Dark Side, Nif. Seriously." Karsten holds his hand to his chest with dramatic flair.

"It's not that big a deal. They were nice. We talked about my dream of being a singer, and they just wanted to know more about me."

"Sounds fishy to me," Zane says.

"Why? Because no one other than the two of you would ever be friends with someone like me?" I snap back.

"Not in this town," Karsten replies.

I know what he's saying has been proven true time and time again. The people in this town are just so set in their ways that it's like a scientific fact that they're pretty much allergic to outsiders. But, right now, I just want so badly for things to be good that I need to believe they've changed, even if I know in my heart they haven't.

My body starts to tingle as my face gets hot, and I yell, "You're just jealous." I run ahead, leaving them both in my wake.

When I get home from school, I slam the front door of the house and avoid looking at my parents, who are both sitting at the dining room table, and I run to my room. Throwing my face into my pillow, I scream.

Why am I here? If life is going to be like this forever, why didn't the car hit me and spare someone who was pretty, popular, worthy of living life? I truly don't understand, and the more I think about it, the deeper and deeper I go into darkness as I cry tears so heavy they soak my pillow within minutes.

I see the man standing next to me. Who was he? I bet he was valuable. Why did *he* die, and I didn't?

I see the paramedics pull the sheet over a body lying in the middle of the street as I make my way to triage. Who was that person? Did they have a family? Were they making a difference? Why am I here, and they're not?

Then I see the little baby with the wires coming out of her tiny little body on the X-ray machine, and I see her parents sob with the news. She was just starting.

What if she would have been the next Mother Teresa? She was clearly more valuable than I am.

I just don't understand why I'm here, and they're not.

My parents knock on the door. "Go away!" I yell. I just can't deal with their looks right now. It only adds to how awful I feel. I wish I could feel great and grateful that I survived, but my body and brain just won't let me. *What a waste*, I think to myself. *Here you are, one of the lucky ones, and you're just wasting your second chance.*

"Nif, we're coming in." My mom gently pushes my bedroom door open.

"No. Please don't," I plead. "I just need to be left alone." I feel guilty enough without them in the room, but they come in anyway.

"It's going to be alright," they say, holding me, which just makes me feel worse. But I know they mean well, so I let them hold me even though I want to kick and scream and push them away.

Stop crying, and they'll leave, I tell myself, working really hard to stop the tears that just want to keep coming. It honestly hurts when they hug me. My skin constantly feels like it's on fire. Like I've got a really bad sunburn. But I don't want to make them feel bad, so I keep quiet and will myself to stop, and it finally ends. My parents leave, and I silently begin to cry into my pillow, pledging to make sure I no longer let anyone see me cry.

Chapter Twelve

"Hey," Zane says as she and Karsten make their way toward my locker.

"Hey." I try to hide my exhaustion. I didn't sleep at all the night before, and I just don't have the energy to deal with another battle with the two of them, even though I still think they're being jealous.

"Listen, sweetie, we feel bad about yesterday, but we're just trying to protect you from the depths of darkness that you were clearly going down." He's obviously assuming I think they were right.

"That's not really an apology, Karsten." The anger I'm feeling rises to the surface. "I don't think they're the pit of darkness, and I liked hanging out with them yesterday!"

"Nif, you can't be serious," Zane responds. "Have you forgotten how awful they've been in the past?"

"They haven't been awful to me. You've only told me stories. How do I even know those stories are true?" I fold my arms and squint my eyes. I'm just so over this.

"Really? You're questioning our honesty and loyalty to you?" Karsten shoots back, dramatically offended.

"Maybe I am." I slam my locker and walk away.

I just can't believe them. I'm finally starting to feel better. I'm finally starting to feel like people might like me. I'm finally feeling the way I have always hoped being a star would make me feel, and they want to take that from me. What kind of friends are they?

Just then, Maggie walks up. "Nif, I want to talk to you." I nod as she continues, "Well, I'm assuming that you saw my announcement yesterday about leaving the show." I nod again. "I was wondering if you would want to take my place?"

"What?" I try to hide my complete and utter excitement. *Keep it cool, Nif.* "Isn't there an audition process?"

"Normally, yes. But we all thought that, since you're having such a hard go of it, we'd just give it to you," Maggie says back with a look of pity I can't ignore.

Ugh, Jessa is right! I think. I can't get where I want on my own merits. Everything I've accomplished has been because of people either feeling sorry for me or because there's no one else who wants to do it. I'm so sick of feeling like whenever I get something, it's because of pity or convenience.

"I'll have to think about it." I watch as her face changes to anger.

"What?" Her face twists in a confused and shocked way. "But we're trying to do something nice for you. Why are you being so ungrateful?"

Her reaction is not something I expected, and I don't know what to say, so I just stand there… a little too long because she grows more angry by the second and then storms off in a huff.

"Wait!" I yell after her. She slows down and turns toward me. "I'm so sorry. I don't know what I was thinking. Of course I want to do it."

"Hhmf," she mutters and flattening her hair as if to compose herself and says, "Well, okay then, that's much better. I'll let the team know that your first day will be next Wednesday."

"Great. Thanks!" I hope to see the pitying look she had on her face earlier. I'll take pity over anger any day. Especially anger from Maggie. The stories Zane and Karsten have told me about her "fits of rage," as Karsten likes to call them, are legendary.

She walks away with a half smile, and I breathe a sigh of relief and at the same time know Zane and Karsten were right, and now I owe them an apology.

Chapter Thirteen

Uh-oh, I think to myself, trying not to let the panic take over as I stare at the words flashing in front of me on the monitor. People are blurs as they hustle about trying to get everything ready for the live broadcast.

I blink my eyes, hoping it's just my focus and that the screen is too far away. I have a printed backup copy of what I'm supposed to say on the table in front of me, and I take a look. Nope. Not the screen. Panic creeps closer to the surface as I feel my chest start to tighten.

"Are you okay?" Zane aggressively whispers in my ear as she squats down next to where I'm sitting. "We go live in five minutes."

"I can't read the words," I admit, trying not to cry. "I just keep reading the same sentence over and over again, but I don't actually know what it says. STOP looking at me like that!" I scream-whisper after looking at the panic starting to form across Zane's face.

"What's up, you two lovelies?" Karsten pretends to fix the makeup on my face, knowing full well both Zane and I are in crisis mode.

"Nif can't read the words," Zane informs him.

"WHAT?" Karsten yells unintentionally and then lowers his voice to a whisper. "What?"

"Yeah, it's been happening a lot lately." I'm pleading for help with my eyes.

"Why didn't you tell us?" they both reply in unison.

"Okay, don't panic. I know what to do." Zane leaves both of us sitting there, looking frantically at each other for guidance, knowing we aren't going to get it from each other.

Zane comes back with an earpiece. "Here," she slams it in my ear, "we bought these last month when we sent Blake to cover the puppy adoption at Miller's hardware store. Just repeat after me."

Karsten and I both look at each other. He shrugs, and I sigh with relief. I don't know what I would do without them.

Fifteen minutes later as the director yells cut, Zane and Karsten both come rushing over. Zane is clearly recovering from being more stressed than I think she's ever been in her entire life as sweat drips down her face. "Why didn't you tell me you couldn't read?" she yell-whispers, her face bright red. "I do not like being caught unprepared."

"I don't know. I guess I just didn't think it was a big deal. Look, everything worked out fine, after all. Thanks for your help." I try to brush off the situation when the truth is I haven't been able to read and understand since the crash. I'm pretty sure my grades are getting to a point where the teachers are going to start calling in my parents, but I don't know what to do, and I don't want to talk about it. No one seems to understand what I'm saying whenever I do talk about it. It's all so strange and unrelatable. I've now been to three different therapists because none of them understand and can help. I have another appointment tomorrow with one I am feeling somewhat hopeful about, but if history is anything, it's probably a baseless hope.

The rest of the crew makes their way to the table where I'm sitting with congratulations and job-well-dones. They seem to be really happy I've joined the team, and for the first time in this godforsaken town, I feel like I belong. I look over toward Zane with a big smile on my face, only to be met with a disapproving look. I know she'll keep my secret, but I also know this isn't the last we will talk about it either.

She leaves, and I turn back to my fellow news peeps.

Chapter Fourteen

I PLOP DOWN ON THE BIG, COMFY, SHABBY-CHIC COUCH set in the middle of the brightly colored office, grab a pillow to hold on to, and settle in. Looking around, I see loads of Eastern-style decorations: a statue of a person meditating, a poster of the chakras, a lotus flower. All things I've only seen when visiting Zane's Nana's apartment. I don't really know what they mean but understand that they are usually around people who are very wise.

A woman in her late forties enters the room with a warm smile. She introduces herself as Sally. I immediately like her. She's not like the others. She's kind and engaged. She has a notebook, but takes very few notes. In addition to the therapist who fell asleep, I've had one who was constantly writing notes with the notebook in front of his face so I couldn't even see if he was listening and one who had such a bad case of post-nasal drip that I came out of that appointment more on edge than when I went in.

This doctor was recommended by Zane's Nana, and I can see the similarities.

"How are you?" she asks in a way that makes me feel like she actually wants to know. It wasn't like the obligatory "how are you," but a get to the heart of the matter "how are you."

"Fine." This has become my normal way of responding. I mean, what am I supposed to say? I'm awful, actually, thanks for asking. Who does that?

"No, really. How are you?" she presses, and I can tell that she isn't going to be one that I easily get through a session with.

"I'm okay." I wish she would just take my word for it.

She doesn't.

"Okay." She just sits there and looks at me.

"Ummm… no, really, I'm fine," I stammer.

"Uh-huh." She just sits there, looking at me some more.

After a few minutes, the awkwardness gets to the point where I can't take the silence. "What do you want me to say?"

"I want you to tell me how you are."

I take a deep breath, trying to hold back the tears that are certainly going to come if I say too much.

"Honestly, I don't know how to explain how I am. I don't know the words."

"Well, now we're getting somewhere." She smiles back.

I feel relief. I feel safe with her. Like, even if she can't relate—I mean, honestly, with something like this, who can?—she's at least making it okay for me to fumble around while I try to find the right words to explain these unexplainable feelings.

"I feel embarrassed, ashamed, conflicted..."

"Okay, that's a great place to start. Why do you feel this way?"

"Well." I gear up to share something I haven't shared with anyone before. "I am embarrassed and ashamed for so many reasons. I mean, the most obvious is the fact that I can't seem to get it together, and I'm crying all the time. But the reason I'm feeling conflicted—everything I say is confidential, right?" I interrupt myself just to be sure before revealing thoughts that make me feel like a truly awful human.

"Yes, everything you say to me is protected under doctor-patient confidentiality unless it is leading to the harm of yourself or someone else."

"Okay. Did you hear the news this morning? The news about how the man who ran us over is being charged with ten counts of grossly negligent vehicular manslaughter."

"No, I hadn't heard about that."

"Yeah, from what I understand, the gross negligence part means he might have done it on purpose. The day of the crash, I remember someone running by saying he did it on purpose, and I honestly don't know how to deal with that. I mean, how could someone just decide to run down four blocks of people? None of this makes sense to me. The part that makes me feel so horrible is that when I heard the news that he was being charged, I felt a little…" I take a big gulp, "better. Like, maybe people will finally understand how this man has truly messed up so many lives. But, at the same time, what if it was an accident, and he didn't mean to do it? I mean, I can't see that being the case, if I'm being honest, because he didn't hit any of the vendors or turn and hit a wall to stop himself. He literally drove until there was nothing left to hit and stopped his car. So, I feel so conflicted, and I don't know how to make sense of any of it." I take a deep breath, realizing I had just said all of that with one breath.

Sally just sits for a minute taking it all in before she says, "It's completely normal to feel this way."

Ugh! I absolutely hate it when people use the word "normal" to explain what I'm feeling. NONE of this is normal! I try not to shut down. I really like Sally, and so far, she's been the best therapist I've had. *You've got to forgive her for not understanding that the word "normal" is so infuriating.* I look up and see from the furrowed brow on her face that she is deep in thought.

"Have you ever tried acupuncture?"

"I don't know what that is," I reply back with curiosity. I haven't felt this—good isn't the right word because I am still far from feeling good, but better works—since the crash, so I am open to anything this magical woman has to say.

"It's a form of ancient Chinese medicine where they place needles…"

"*Needles?!* Yeah, nope. Nuh-uh. I do not voluntarily do things that involve needles." I push back.

She laughs. "That's a pretty standard response. But, if you'll let me finish, I think you'll find great relief and benefit from the treatment."

Relief, I think to myself. Relief is all I want in life right now. At the beginning, I wanted to be back to the way I was before, but now, now, after not sleeping for months, relief sounds great.

Sally rips a prescription out of her little pad and hands it to me. "Go see Dr. Taka and tell him I sent you. I'll see you next week."

With that, I have a new therapist.

Chapter Fifteen

Sitting on the acupuncturist's table, I feel like a zombie, a shell of what I used to be. I haven't slept a full eight hours in about three months now, and I don't even have the energy to fake being fine anymore. I'm desperate. I *need* this to work. Even a little calm would be magical. Magic, do I even believe in that anymore? I used to. I really did. I believed that if you put out good energy, it would come back. When I heard one of my favorite celebrities describe energy that way, it made sense to me. I identified it as magic. But what energy was I putting out into the world that was so bad that this happened to me?

The acupuncturist, a sweet elderly man, is speaking to me in soft, calming tones, but I can't understand what he's saying. He sounds like the teacher in the old Charlie Brown cartoons my parents used to watch while talking about how they don't make 'em like they used to. The voice was just a series of wha-wha-whas with no real words. Yep, that's what this guy sounds like.

He gently puts his hand on my shoulder as he guides me to my bed. I am so exhausted and out of it, I barely remember that there are needles involved. Then the first one is in. *Hmmm… did he just poke me with a needle?* I think to myself. *I didn't feel that at all. What is this quackery? I mean, shouldn't I at least feel something?*

"Okay, now you just relax, and I'll be back in a little while to check on you." He closes the door gently as he exits the room.

The needles are in already? I think, *Yep, I could tell*, as I lift my hand up to see several poking out of my skin. *I don't think this is going to wo… what the heck?* I think as the floodgates open, my body shaking lightly like a lightbulb flickering on and off as it dies out. Sobs now, uncontrollable… *Where the heck is this coming from?* It doesn't feel at all emotional, more like my body is just releasing some seriously intense energy. *I'm not sure how I feel about this,* I think as another wave of sobs and shakes hit me. I give in and sob myself into a calm, relaxing sleep.

I gently open my eyes as I feel the acupuncturist removing needles. "What happened?" I ask, feeling groggy. He gently smiles at me.

"You tell me," he says, pulling more needles out than I realized he had put in.

"Well, when you left, I suddenly burst into tears without any thoughts, and that lasted until I fell asleep."

"That's perfectly normal and due to several points. The most prominent is this one." He points to a spot just below my throat. "That one tends to help us release pent-up energy."

"Well, I clearly have a lot of that," I say, feeling noticeably more energetic than when I arrived.

"Yes," he says matter-of-factly. "You've definitely got some work to do."

I can't help it as the tears come like a river again. I'm exhausted at the idea of having to do more.

"I'm so tired," I sob.

"I know. But your reaction today shows that this is a treatment that will most likely work for you. It will take some time, but have hope, my dear." He has such a kind voice.

I breathe a sigh of relief and resolve to add this to my therapies. I'm too tired to even be frustrated at this point.

Chapter Sixteen

ONE OF MY FAVORITE SMELLS SURPRISES ME AS I WALK through the door and smile with delight. It's been an insanely long day, and the comforting smell of my mom's homemade spaghetti sauce is just what the doctor ordered. I walk towards the kitchen in a daze led by the aroma, just like in one of those old Looney Tunes cartoons my parents still love to watch on Saturday. I'm just now realizing how many cartoons my parents still watch. Interesting. Anyway, I see my mom standing over the pot stirring the sauce. It's a secret family recipe, and it takes all day, so it must be a special occasion.

"Hey, Mom, what's the occasion?"

"No occasion, I just know it's your favorite and thought I'd make it for you."

I hug her without even thinking about it. I am just so grateful these days for any small things to spark that ever-increasing unfamiliar feeling of joy. This happened to me once before when my dog died in fourth grade. The pain was so intense, and I couldn't stop thinking about her. It was constant. She would just pop into my head all the time. Eventually, it got to the point where I would have to trigger a thought of her by looking at a photo or going to the park where we used to play fetch.

Never in my wildest dreams did I think it could go that way with happiness. Like, right now, I need a diligent trigger in order to feel joy. It doesn't just come to me. It's so dark in my head that only triggers from before the crash bring me joy. Like the smell of my mom's spaghetti sauce.

I walk to my room, feeling grateful for her and excited to eat!

"I'm going to do my homework." But I know full well that means I'm going to stay in my room staring at the same line of text for like twenty minutes, trying to understand what the heck I'm reading, get frustrated, throw the book on the floor, and scream into my pillow. This is my new nightly routine. I do approach it with hope most days, but today I'm so exhausted that just the thought of those twenty minutes makes me want to run away from home. But, as my therapist keeps reminding me, all I can do is try. So, try I will.

A knock on the door startles me awake.

"Nif, dinner's ready," my mom announces through the door.

"Okay, be right there," I respond, rubbing my eyes. Hard as I tried, I was right. The homework led to frustrated crying, but my exhaustion overtook it, and I ended up asleep. Exhausted naps are really the only non-nightmare-filled sleep I get lately. I'm not sure if that means I'm getting better sleep when I take naps, or if I just don't get to the deep sleep where we dream. All I know is I don't know what to do.

Just then, I remember the spaghetti and hop out of bed with a little pep in my step. Gosh, I'm excited for tonight's meal. My plan is to focus all conversation on Mom's delicious meal and avoid any talk of me, homework, what's going on with my stupid PTSD, or anything like that. It has completely taken over my life, and my family still just does not understand. I'm too tired to try to explain why my grades are falling, or what's happening with yet another new therapy I'm trying. And, honestly, all I want to do is eat.

"Wow. Look at this." I walk toward the dining room table. "Everything looks so nice."

"Thanks! I did it all myself." Jane's face is beaming with pride. "I figured even though there was no special occasion, per se," (another term she that she's been using non-stop), "Mom's spaghetti is occasion enough."

We all laugh in agreement, and I'm impressed she's really understanding how to use the term *per se* correctly.

"Mom, this smells incredible." I let the aroma permeate my nose. "Mmmmmmm."

"Well, I had time today and figured you could use a little pick-me-up with everything going on…"

Uh-oh, it's starting already. Please don't ask me how things are going. I just can't.

"How are things going anyway? I know you had another doctor's appoint…"

I interrupt. "They're fine. How long did it take to cook this sauce?" I ask, knowing full well it takes eight hours, but hoping she'll dive into explaining the process even though we've all heard it a million times. She does, and I take a bite of my spaghetti, feeling relieved. It then hits me how good it is; the smell when it goes past my nose is just the start. The taste of the tomato and oregano and all the spices transports me back to being a kid at my grandma's house. The texture of the noodles feels so good in my mouth as I chew, and I'm in a different world. The only thing about the sauce is that I always have to add something. So, as is my traditional way of eating, I take the first bite, have my moment of euphoria, and then say, "Could you please pass the…" I stop short. *What is that word again?* "Could you please pass the…" *What the heck?!?*

I can see what I need sitting right in the middle of the table. I know what it is, but can't for the life of me remember the word. It's as if the sentence is typed out in my brain, but someone has taken a big black sharpie and covered up the word I'm trying to get out of my mouth. As hard as I try to focus, I just can't see it. To the shock of my family, tears start to explode from my eyes. *Why is my brain doing this? When am I going to get better? Am I really going to be this way forever? I don't know if I can handle it.* These are all thoughts going through my head as my mom comes and squats down beside me.

"What is going on?" she asks in complete confusion. She really doesn't understand, and the problem is that I don't either, and if I can't remember a simple word, how am I supposed to explain what is happening in my head?

"Salt," I whisper into her shoulder through my tears. "Please pass the salt."

Chapter Seventeen

The next day, my mom comes into my room and exclaims, "Today, we're playing hooky!"

"Wait, what? I have a math test, and I've already missed so much school."

"Yes, that may be true, but you haven't really just relaxed during that time off." I know my mom has the best intentions, but she just doesn't seem to understand that relaxing for me, right now, isn't possible. My body is so tense that it hurts if someone bumps into me at school, hugs hurt (which, as a hugger, makes me super sad, but that's a topic for another time), and even the thought of having a day where the goal is to relax makes me feel more stress than I can express.

But, after looking at her face and seeing the "this is absolutely going to be the solution to me getting my daughter back on track" look, I give in.

"Okay, what's the plan?" I ask with as big a smile as I can muster—which, for the record, is probably the size of a jelly bean.

"Well, do you remember my friend Beth? She lives about two towns over." I nod. "Okay, good, you remember." She's being kind of suspicious. "I was thinking we could go visit Beth, ride some horses, have a little lunch, and then you could talk to her husband, who is a psychiatrist."

"Wait, what?" I was nodding along until we got to the psychiatrist part. "Mom, we talked about this! I don't want to take medication. That stuff is addictive, and after what happened with Grandpa, I know I'm more at risk, and, besides, when they gave me a sleeping pill right after the crash, it made me feel funny and… ugh. I just don't want to! Just leave me alone. I'm going to go to school." I turn over in bed so my back is to her.

"Nif, I know all this is scary, but so is the fact that you're not sleeping. The school called a couple days ago, and we know your grades have dropped to scary levels. If you don't do something, you might not graduate."

"Mom, that's not true. I've already got enough credits to graduate."

"Okay, then, if you don't do something, we'll need to talk to Mrs. M and pull you from the concert."

"You'd do that?" I turn back toward her in order to look her right in the eye. "Take away the one thing that is bringing me joy at the moment? The only time I feel like I'm not trapped in a nightmare. You'd take that away from me?"

"If we have to, to get you to try medication so you can sleep, yeah. We would. It's what's best for you."

"You mean it's what's best for *you*. So you don't have to worry! So you can feel better! What's best for me is to sing."

I'm stubborn, but my mom is more stubborn, and I know it. She's also got the advantage of multiple full nights of sleep on her side, so all I can do is give in.

We ride in silence, but my head is loud. I'm so pissed. I can't believe I'm going to have to take medication; just the thought of it is causing even more stress. But it all subsides when we pull up to Beth's house. I open the car door, and the smell of fresh-cut hay and the neighing of horses overcome me, and I forget everything I was thinking about.

"Hi, Beth." I walk past her as if in a trance on my way to pet Apple, my favorite horse of all time.

"Hi, girl. It's been too long." I reach out and pull her face toward mine. We nuzzle for a second as she sniffs. "Ahhh, is this what you want?" I pull an apple from my coat pocket. She eats, and we look into each other's eyes. She seems to understand, and I am unbelievably grateful for the connection to this majestic creature.

Mom and Beth walk up behind me.

"Apple's been excited all morning since I told her you were coming to see her," Beth says.

"She's just the best!" I respond, my eyes still locked with hers.

"Well, let's saddle her up." Beth starts walking toward the barn, and I run to catch up.

A few minutes later, we're all moseying through the woods on our horses. I'm a little further ahead, leaning down onto Apple's neck as my head bops up and down with each step she takes. There is nothing like the feeling of riding a horse.

"I don't know why it's taken me so long to come and see you, my friend," I whisper to Apple as she carries me through the woods. "You are exactly what I needed. My parents took my license away last week because I fell asleep and drove into a ditch, but once I get it back, I'm going to visit you all the time. Would that be okay?" Apple tosses her head back as if she agrees that it's a good idea. I laugh as my mom and Beth gallop up next to me.

"Getting along well, I see," Mom says, slowing to match Apple's pace.

"Apple just loves you, Nif. You definitely have to come and visit her more," Beth innocently offers, not knowing about the license thing.

Mom shifts in her seat and looks at me and then Beth. "Hopefully, after this meeting with Henry, that might be possible."

"Oh, right, I completely forgot." Beth looks at her watch. "He should be home any minute. We should head back so we can get you taken care of."

We all begin to head back, only this time I'm behind Mom and Beth. I don't want my time on Apple to end, and I don't want to talk to Henry.

As we arrive back at Beth's place, I see Henry pulling in.

"Perfect timing," Beth says as she dismounts from her horse. "Your mom and I will take care of the horses. You can go on up to the house to meet with Henry."

I say my goodbyes to Apple by nuzzling her nose again. I give her the apple from my other coat pocket as a thank you, and I begrudgingly hand over the reins to my mom.

It's going to be fine, I think to myself. *I mean, the statistics aren't 100 percent, and I've beat statistics before. I can do this. And who knows? Maybe the medication will be good. Maybe I'll finally get some sleep. Henry's a great person too, so it's not like he's going to do something to hurt me. Just be okay with this.* "No, seriously, be okay with this!" I yell to myself as I walk through the door.

There's this old '80s sitcom where the dad is a therapist with his office right off the front door of their house. Henry's office reminds me of this show, and Henry reminds me of that dad. He's sort of goofy but not to the point that you don't trust him. Anyway, I also always thought it was weird that some therapists have offices in their homes. *Doesn't that mess with doctor-patient confidentiality? I mean, isn't it a problem that Beth knows he sees me? What if he tells her what's going on with me? Oh, please, like Mom's not already doing that. Stop!* I tell myself. *He's a good person who's trying to help you. Just go with it. Just…*

"Hi, Nif," Henry breaks my thought spiral, "I'm happy to see you."

Are you? That's a weird thing to say to someone you're about to put on drugs. You're doing it again. I pull myself out of this potential thought spiral with a "Hi."

His office *really* does remind me of that '80s sitcom I was telling you about. Probably because it looks like he opened it in the '80s and hasn't decorated it since.

"Have a seat." He points to a white loveseat with giant pink-and-teal flowers and a lace ruffle. *It's kind of tragic,* I think trying to distract myself from what's about to happen…

"So, tell me what's been going on." Henry moves to get comfortable with his notepad on his lap and pen in his hand.

Yup, there it is. The dreaded "tell me what's happening" line. I'm so sick of telling people what happened. Can't they just assume it's awful and fix me without me having to relive it over and over again? Wishful thinking on my part.

"Well…" I begin to tell the story.

About half an hour later (I've figured out at this point what's important for the doctors to hear and what's not, so I sort of have a CliffsNotes version), Henry is looking at me with that familiar "I'm so sorry" look.

"It's fine," I assert, trying to snap him out of it. "What's next?"

"Well, I think we'll try flurazepam and see what happens." He writes on his prescription pad, rips it out, hands it to me, and says, "Take this tonight and call me tomorrow and let me know if it worked."

"We can know that quickly?" I ask.

"Yep, it should work right away. But know that this is a process, so definitely call me tomorrow so we can make sure it's the right medication."

"Okay, I will." I'm feeling both hope and dread at the same time. I'm real sick of this "process," but I'm also hopeful that this will work, and the fact that I'll know tonight is so cool.

"Well, how'd it go?" Mom asks as we get into the car.

"Fine." I try not to give her any satisfaction. "I have to take this medication tonight before bed and call Henry in the morning to tell him how it went. Now,

I did what you asked. I can still sing in the concert, right?"

"Yes, Nif, you can still sing in the concert," she replies, knowing what I'm doing. "Thank you for doing this."

We drive home in silence, but I'm actually feeling hopeful.

Chapter Eighteen

How can this little tiny pill make everything better? I think as I roll the pinkish-colored pill around in my hand, quietly hoping with all my might that it will actually work.

"Nif, did you take your pill?" my mom yells from the living room. I cringe with embarrassment. Like, I know everyone in the house knows because my mom just couldn't help but share all the details. We just had to fill it in town even though I begged her to go somewhere where they didn't know us. I hate that she's okay with everyone knowing all our business. It's hard enough to deal with living in this hellhole. To do it with all this extra stuff going on is almost unbearable. But I'm just too tired to fight at this point, so I yell back…

"Yes, Mom! I'm taking it right now."

I beg and plead with my brain, one last time, *Please work! Please work! Please work!* and I swallow hard as a tear of frustration and hope streams down my cheek. I wipe it away and yell goodnight to everyone as I climb in bed and sink under the covers with an exhausted heart, clinging to that hope with every fiber of my being.

That hope is crushed when I wake up in panic a couple hours later, my heart racing, tears stinging as they roll freely from my eyes. I try not to hyperventilate because that's loud, and, well, frankly, it hurts. I don't want to wake anyone up. I can't believe it didn't work. I let the tears that started from the nightmare I just woke up from come hard as they turn into tears of realization that the nightmare I'm living is my reality. It doesn't matter if I'm asleep or awake; it's all the same. One giant nightmare.

But, if my parents find out the medication isn't working, they won't let me sing, and I can't have that. Singing is the only time I feel normal and good. I decide that I will tell them I slept. I mean, it's not a complete lie. I did sleep a couple hours longer than normal. Maybe it's enough?

I take a sip of water and lie back down in my bed. With my eyes closed, I try to will myself back to sleep. I'm so tired. It doesn't make any sense that I'm not sleeping. "Why?" I ask myself, and then a flash of people lying in the street comes across my eyelids, and I'm reminded why. No matter how tired I am, I don't want to see dead people anymore. So, I open my eyes and just lie there not knowing what to do.

As the sun creeps through the blinds in my bedroom, I look over at the clock. It's 6 a.m., and I feel like it's safe to get out of bed without arousing suspicion. All the hours staring at the ceiling gave me an opportunity to come up with a plan.

I'm definitely going to tell my parents the pills worked. I mean, what's the worst that can happen, right? It's not like I haven't already been living with this for months now. It can't possibly get worse, and I'm doing pretty OKAY considering. And, again, I did get two extra hours of sleep. More than I've gotten in a long time. So, maybe a few nights in a row of, like, four to six hours will start to make me feel better. I don't know. What I do know is that if I tell them it's not working, it means more doctor's visits, different pills with who-knows-what kind of side effects, and more attention put on what's wrong with me. Most of all, there's the possibility that they won't let me sing in the concert. I just can't take it anymore.

I muster up the energy to get dressed, put on a smile, and open my door. No one is awake yet, so my smile immediately disappears. I make breakfast as a way to prove I'm fine, and it seems to work.

Everyone comes to the dining room table to eat. My mom's smile as she greets me proves that she is happy with what she sees. "Looks like the pills worked. You seem chipper this morning."

"Yeah, they seem to." I mean, technically, it's not a lie. I didn't say they *did* work. I just confirmed what she thought by using the word *seem.* So, I'm in the clear.

After breakfast, I bolt out of the house with a, "Gotta go. Early choir practice. Love you. Bye," knowing if I don't leave right now, I won't be able to hold it together.

Chapter Nineteen

I LOOK OVER AT JESSA TRYING TO KEEP HER BALANCE as she practices her piece for tryouts while doing the most awkward little spin. "She's so lame," I think, trying not to be distracted by my annoyance with her. I wish she would get out of my head, but ever since her snarky comment about how *she* is clearly the most valuable asset to the choir this morning, I've been burning with rage. The rage is getting harder to control the less I sleep, but I am holding onto the fact that I absolutely have to control myself, or I won't get to sing in the concert, whether I get this solo or not. So, I focus on my own practice. I mean, this solo has some serious soul, which Jessa just doesn't have. She's good and all, but more of a classic-type singer. I definitely have the ability to emote, and that's something she just can't seem to do. If only I can keep it together long enough to get through this audition *and* nail the choreography I've been working on the past couple of weeks, I have a really good shot.

"All right, everyone!" Mrs. M flies into the room with a loud clap! clap! clap! that breaks my concentration and nearly sends me into a panic attack. *Breathe deep. You're okay,* I tell myself, calming my nervous system as best I can. It's getting harder and harder to control my body because of the lack of sleep, but it somehow knows that not having a panic attack right now is a matter of life and death for me. I'll simply die if I can't sing, so it stays calm on the outside. This type of self-control hurts so much, but I'm able to hold it together and put on a smile for Mrs. M.

"Is everyone ready for the tryouts?" she asks enthusiastically and is met with the same enthusiasm from the four of us that are trying out. The other two girls in the room are freshmen, so they're not really competition. They're more there to get the experience of trying out. Jessa and I are seniors and have priority unless they are really just that much better than us.

"Okay, Nif, let's start with you." My face grows red as I walk to my spot next to the piano where I normally try out but remember as I'm walking up that I need to be a bit away in order to do the dance part. *Don't worry. No one noticed. You're going to be great. You've been practicing for weeks. It's all good. You got this.*

The sound of the piano breaks me from my trance as I take a deep breath. "Ready when you are."

Mrs. M begins to play.

"Loves to hear the music blasting up to the sky," I sing in my most soulful voice while nailing the choreography I'd just been practicing. I get done with a genuine smile on my face, knowing I laid it all out there. I absolutely did my best, and even though I'm exhausted from not sleeping, the rush of performing outweighs the exhaustion as I make my way back to my chair.

I sit patiently and respectfully as Jessa and the other two girls audition.

Mrs. M goes to her office with a, "Be right back. Please wait here."

"Well, *Nif…*" Ugh, Jessa and that grating voice. I seriously can't stand her.

"Yes?" I reply with as much calm as I can muster.

"Congrats on doing the best you could do, given your situation."

"What does that mean, Jessa?" I ask, knowing better.

"I mean, my mom saw *your* mom picking up your prescription from your psychiatrist." She leans in and whispers the word *psychiatrist* so that the other girls can absolutely hear her, even though it looks like she's trying to be discreet.

"Whatever, Jessa." I do not have the energy to deal with her, and I don't know what to say as my face begins to feel hot and beads of sweat start to form on the back of my neck. Thank goodness they're forming there beneath my hair so no one can see them.

Mrs. M comes in just then, and all the focus shifts to her as I breathe a sigh of relief. God, I would do anything to never have to be in the same room as Jessa again.

"You all did a great job. However, one of you not only did a great job with the solo, but a particularly great job choreographing your dance routine, and that's why, Nif, I'd like for you to sing the solo and choreograph the entire song, if you're up for it."

"Absolutely!" I respond, so excited I can barely contain myself. All feeling of exhaustion leaves my body at that moment.

"Yeah, if she doesn't have another *episode,*" Jessa mumbles under her breath.

I can tell everyone heard it, but Mrs. M ignores it and throws out her hands to welcome me to the middle of the room next to her.

"The rest of you, will, of course, be singing the group parts of the song so you, along with the rest of the show choir, will be learning Nif's choreography. Nif, we only have three weeks until showtime, so I hope you're ready to share the dance moves with the rest of the group."

"No problem." I notice that my face hurts from smiling so hard. I smile even bigger when I see how annoyed Jessa is by this news. It's a great moment. I know it's petty, but I don't care.

Chapter Twenty

"Come on, you guys! Get it together! We've been rehearsing this for two weeks straight. It's not that hard, and the concert's only a week away," I yell, unable to control my frustration anymore after Paul and Rebecca collide once again.

I mean, seriously, I haven't slept more than a couple hours a night in months, and these people can't string two simple dance moves together. I honestly don't know how they got their spots on the show choir. Amateurs.

"Let's do it again!" I holler with as much pep and supportive energy as I can muster. Which at this point, I know, is very little.

Everyone groans as Jessa pipes in with her two cents. "Nif, it's not like it's Broadway. God, lighten up."

The thing is it *is* as important to me as if the Tony committee were coming to see it. It's my last shot at redemption. If I don't get this right, I'm never getting out of here, and the thought of being stuck in *Karlville* for the rest of my life is too hard to bear. "You know what, Jessa…" I start to gear up to lay into her when Mrs. M walks in.

"How's it going, everyone?" she asks in a completely cheerful tone, unaware of what's going on.

"Nif has lost her mind," Jessa whines. "And I'm not talking about all the crap that's been happening since the crash. I'm talking about her choreographing this number. She's driving us all crazy with her demands."

"You know what?" I'm unable to hold back my anger anymore. "I can't work with these amateurs anymore. It's not that hard, and they just keep messing it up! I just… I just… I can't." I stutter to express the sheer emotions I'm feeling. "I'm done."

With that, I turn and leave the room.

On the other side of the door, I run right into Zane. I look up at her startled face, and the tears just come. She grabs my hand and rushes me into the bathroom.

"What happened?" she asks as she grabs some toilet paper from the stall and starts wiping away the stream of tears that just won't stop.

"I'm… I'm… I'm… trying so hard, you know?" I struggle to get the words out between the sobs. "I mean, why can't they see that I'm only trying to make us all look the best we can? It's like they don't even care. Why are they even in the choir if they don't care about looking like idiots? Which is what they look like. I mean, Jessa couldn't dance her way out of a paper bag, and Paul and Rebecca spend more time running into each other than actually getting the steps right. UGH, I just don't get it!"

Zane just looks at me, the way she does when she's about to lay a truth bomb on me, and I just put my hand out. "STOP. I know what you're going to say, but I'm sorry. You just don't get how important this is." And, with that, I wipe my eyes and walk out of the bathroom.

I know Zane is only trying to help, but she just doesn't get it, and I'm so tired of trying to explain it. Choir and singing are my only ways out of this place. A place she thinks is perfectly fine but a place that makes me feel like the biggest loser on the planet. I can't explain to her and have her understand that, before the crash, it felt like my soul was constantly screaming at me. Now I have this constant feeling of panic that is getting harder and harder to suppress, *and* don't know whether or not I'm going to graduate because my brain just doesn't work the way it used to.

All these things are making everything seem more and more dire, but no one, and I mean no one, understands. And I don't want to burden anyone with my poor sob story either, so why can't everyone in choir just flipping do their jobs?!

I leave the bathroom and walk past the choir room when I hear Mrs. M shout from inside, "Nif, would you come in here, please?"

My shoulders slump, and I walk in to face the music.

An hour later, I walk out feeling a little better. Mrs. M, knowing each choir member's strengths and weaknesses, helped me rework the choreography so that everyone could succeed and we would all look amazing on the night of the show. She had already asked the choir to come back for an emergency rehearsal after school, and with the show only a week away, I was nervous that the group couldn't get it together. Still, I know there is hope because Mrs. M knows everyone so well and she seems to think it will all work out. It makes me feel good that they are all willing to come back and try again, even though I completely lost it on them.

Chapter Twenty-One

Ugh, stop! Stop! Everything is going to be fine! I try and get myself to stop fidgeting with my outfit. It's like I can't stop. Life is so out of control that I just can't stop trying to fix the things that I can control, like wiping my hand down my skirt to try and keep it straight even though it's a moot cause. The sounds backstage, as much as I absolutely love them, tonight are so loud and overwhelming they form an unbearable ringing in my ears, and I can't think. I fight the panic knowing that, once we're on stage, the performance will take me away to a place where none of this exists, and for a brief moment, I will find peace.

"Places, everyone. Places." Ahhh, music to my ears. The moment we've all been waiting for. I walk out onto the stage, making sure to avoid the platforms set up sporadically for some of the dancers to dance on and take my place. I am, luckily, not one who has to do the dance on a 4x4 platform. Once we're all in place, we strike our poses as the curtain goes up and the lights slam on, illuminating our special red-and-green bedazzled holiday outfits. The band begins to play, and we break out into song and dance with giant smiles on our faces. We are three numbers away from my solo, and I can't wait to show everyone that I have it together enough to not only get through this performance, but to completely rock it out.

I'm in heaven as the lights blind me to the audience, and I am just in my own little world. Until… I step forward to do my solo, and the spotlight moves just enough for me to catch a glimpse of Karen Kolby, the reporter I was going to meet the day of the crash when, suddenly… I can't breathe. I drop to the ground and am back at the farmers' market. The smell of the car exhaust as it swerves away from me, the sight of the smashed honey, the pain of the table nearly breaking my leg as it gets crushed.

I can still see and hear my classmates and the audience gasp, but I can't get out of the flashback as I'm brought back in at the sight of the elderly woman with the steel-blue eyes, her head surrounded by blood. I want so badly to be able to tell everyone who has now gathered around me that I'm fine; I'll get through it. I know it's not actually happening right now, that it's a flashback, but the flashback takes over. I scream and start to hyperventilate, gasping for air. I can see the absolute panic on Mrs. M's face as she cradles my head, yelling for someone to call 911.

"No, I don't need that," I try to say, but I am trapped in my head, unable to communicate. It's scary, but I've had one of these happen every day since the crash, and I now know that they will pass. I have just been able to hide them from others for the most part. The hyperventilating hurts, and the images are terrifying as I succumb to the darkness that is rushing over me, and I pass out.

I wake up to the paramedics loading me onto a gurney. "I don't need this!" I plead. "This happens to me every day."

My parents are at my side now, and I can see the look of shock on my mom's face. "Nif, what are you talking about?" I don't have the energy to talk, so I lie there silently, thinking I'll deal with this all later.

I can't hold it in anymore. I start to sob. I sob because I've ruined the show, I sob because I feel so embarrassed that I haven't gotten better, I sob because I've clearly put everyone in the audience through a traumatic event. I sob, honestly, because I am beyond tired, and I don't have control over my body.

As they load me into the ambulance, I close my eyes and let the tears come.

Later that night, I'm lying in bed, wide awake. How is it possible for my body not to succumb to the exhaustion and sleep? The nights are the worst, and every time I close my eyes, I am right back to some terrifying part of the crash. But, given how tired I am, I really can't understand how I don't just pass out.

At this point, I am more tired than I have ever been in my life but still cannot get to sleep. *Wait! You have sleeping pills. Maybe you just need to take more of them than you have been. Maybe then they'll work.* I think. I quietly get out of bed so I don't wake anyone up. I'm so tired of being the cause of all this stress.

I go to the bathroom to look for the pills. I open the medicine cabinet, but I don't see them. *That's strange,* I think to myself, *Maybe Mom put them in the drawer.* I open the top drawer—nothing. Then I open the middle drawer—nothing. I open the bottom drawer in a bit of a panic and still nothing. *Where are they? I really need them. I have to get some sleep.* "Maybe they're in the kitchen." I make my way toward the most likely cupboard. Still nothing. With each cupboard door I open, I get less and less careful about being quiet. The panic and tears start to take over, and I begin slamming the doors, going back through the places I've already looked, this time not being as careful as I begin to throw silverware and dishes to the ground, crying hysterically. I'm unable to control myself when my dad walks in and turns on the light.

"Sweetheart, what are you doing?" he asks with a sound of heightened concern I rarely hear out of my dad's mouth.

"I am looking for the sleeping pills! I need to go to sleep!" I scream with desperation.

"Oh, honey," he says, with such compassion that it jolts me out of what I was doing. I stop and look around to just now realize what I have done. The kitchen is completely torn apart. There is cereal all over the floor, a bag of rice has burst open at my feet, and pasta boxes and dried beans are everywhere.

I look up at my dad, and in a moment of clarity, I state in a matter-of-fact tone, "I need to go to the hospital."

He just nods, not truly understanding what I'm going through, but understanding that if I had found those sleeping pills, I would have taken the entire bottle.

Chapter Twenty-Two

It is really late, and the psychiatric unit of the hospital is quiet as I sit alone in an exam room curtained off from the rest of the floor. My dad and I came together while my mom and sister stayed home. I asked my dad if we could spare them this part. He and my mom only agreed after I had started to panic again at the thought of being an even bigger burden than I already was. My dad is off dealing with paperwork, and I am sitting alone with my scary, annoying, "I wish they would go away" thoughts.

"It's going to be okay," I am telling myself over and over in an effort to drown out the thoughts I am having. *Why are you so stupid? Why can't you just pull yourself together? It's not like what you went through was that bad. I mean, you didn't go to war or anything.*

My dad comes running in and grabs my hand. "What are you doing?" he says with exasperation. I look down to see that I have deep scratches on my arm. I haven't even realized I was doing it.

The doctor sees them and, with the kindest eyes, looks at me and says, "Okay, Nif, let's get those bandaged up, and I'll show you to your room."

I just nod.

Looking at my bandaged arm, I think, *How did I get here?* My roommate, a woman I haven't met yet, stirs in her bed as a chill runs up my spine. It's cold in the room, and the only light is a flicker from the hallway exit sign hung above a door that reads, "No eloping." *Why would they need to tell people not to run off and get married in the psych ward?* I think to myself, trying not to cry anymore. I can't fight the thoughts that this woman who now lies twenty feet away might stab me in my sleep. I guess I just need to trust that my parents wouldn't put me somewhere where that could happen as the medication kicks in, and I am taken into a delightful sleep.

The next morning, I sit up and stretch for a minute and then realize where I am. *Not bad,* I think to myself as I look around the room. It's a lot less intimidating seeing the place in the daylight. I yawn as I realize that's the first restful night's sleep I've had in four months. *Holy crap! Am I better?* I think excitedly to myself.

"Hey!" I hear a woman say as she walks through the open door from the hallway, carrying shower supplies.

With her hair up in a towel, she shuffles into the room in her slippers. "I'm Claire." She reaches her hand out as she approaches.

"I'm Jennifer, but everyone calls me Nif." I lean in to shake her hand.

"What are you in for?" she asks as if it's just another interaction, and we're on the street, not in the looney bin.

This is really weird, I think to myself, but answer her anyway. "I've been diagnosed with PTSD," I respond. She sort of chuckles, and I don't know why.

"You say that like you don't believe it. In this place, it's better to fake belief even if you don't, or you'll never get out of here." She turns to leave with a, "See you later."

What the heck was that? I think to myself. *Okay, this woman clearly seems to know what she's talking about. How do I fake that I believe what's going on? I'm going to have to figure this all out because clearly, I don't belong here. I feel so much better. It's obvious that I'm not crazy; I just needed sleep, and I got it. So, maybe they'll let me go home. I should find the doctor. Am I going to get to see the doctor? I don't like not knowing what is happening! Aaahhhh… Okay, calm down. You just woke up. First things first, find the bathroom, and then you can figure everything else out. Right. Good plan, Nif. Good plan.*

Sliding the assigned slippers on, I get out of bed in search of the bathroom.

"Hi, Jennifer," I hear a woman dressed in a nurse's uniform say as I come out of the bathroom.

"Oh, you can call me Nif," I reply back.

"Okay, noted. Let me show you around really quick before your meeting with Dr. Anthony."

I feel a little jolt of butterflies surge through my body. I am feeling so much better from my night's sleep that I am going to ask Dr. Anthony if I can go home. "I don't want to waste your time. I am feeling much better and think I'll be going home today."

She smiles in a sort of patronizing way. "That's wonderful, but my boss will not be okay with me defying her orders, so let me show you around anyway."

I shrug and follow her out the door. The floor that the psych ward is on is oval in shape. I see the door with the "no eloping" sign on it at one end and the nurse's station at the other. There's a smoking room since people on the psych ward aren't allowed outside unless they get special permission, which I'm told is really difficult to get. There's a TV room, but I feel really uncomfortable as we walk by it. It sort of reminds me of a prison show where only the most dangerous of those locked up hang out. I shiver and look away. There's a cafeteria, a group therapy room, and a room that I've decided I'm going to spend most of my time in—an art therapy room. It's practically empty as we walk by, and that alone makes me want to hang out in there. From what I can tell, there are about twenty other patients and ten rooms. It is a full house.

"And the last stop on our tour is Dr. Anthony's office." The nurse motions for me to go in. Another jolt of excitement runs through my body as I take a seat in Dr. Anthony's office. The nurse closes the door as I look around. Clearly, Dr. Anthony loves football. There are photos of professional football players captured doing incredible athletic feats, a bronze football on his desk, ribbons and plaques, and photos of him when he was in high school or maybe college with his team.

He clearly loves the sport. I know nothing about football, so I'm not sure we're going to be able to relate. *I really hope he's not some dumb jock who doesn't understand how important it is for me to get back to my life and get back to performing with the choir*, I think to myself when the door opens and Dr. Anthony walks in.

I straighten up and clear my throat and say with as much authority as I can, "I'd like to go home. I slept really well last night and am feeling better. So, I see no need to stay here any longer."

"Hi, Nif. I'm Dr. Anthony. It's nice to meet you," he says to me as if he didn't hear a word I just said. "I hear you," he continues. *Oh*, I think. *I guess he did hear me. But then why would he go through the formalities?*

I think as he is still talking. Since I was thinking, I missed most of what he said until I hear the words, "Therefore, I think you will need to stay at least forty-eight more hours."

"WHAT?!" The words come out louder than I would have liked. "But I feel better. Staying any longer is unnecessary."

"How long has it been since you got a full night's sleep?" he asks.

"Well, since the crash," I reply.

"Nif, that was four months ago," he responds. "One good night's sleep is not enough to make up for that long of a period of not only not sleeping, but having night terrors, flashbacks, panic attacks… your body has been through a lot. Not to mention your mind. Healing from this type of trauma is going to take a long time. PTSD is no jo…"

I interrupt him with, "I just don't think I have PTSD, doctor. I mean, I'm not a soldier, and what I went through was so quick. It doesn't make sense that I would respond in such an intense way."

"Nif, you don't have to be a soldier in order to experience trauma, and everybody is different, so the severity of the trauma will manifest differently for everyone, and in my, and other doctors', professional opinions, you are not only suffering from PTSD, you are suffering from a severe, debilitating case. And that takes time and specific treatment to heal from."

I go to get ready to defend my POV when I realize he just said *heal.* "Wait, did you just say I can heal from PTSD?" I ask, completely gobsmacked. "Because the doctor that initially diagnosed me said I'd have to deal with this the rest of my life, which basically feels like a life sentence."

"Oh goodness." He looks straight into my eyes with a gaze that pulls me in like a tractor beam. "I'm so sorry you've been carrying that part of your diagnosis around for four months. PTSD is absolutely treatable. You must have felt hopeless this whole time."

"Well, yeah," I respond, sort of annoyed. "I mean, who wants to have nightmares and flashbacks every day for the rest of their lives?"

"Well, it's treatable, but, again, it takes time. So, you need to commit to doing the work."

Ummmm, is that a challenge? Did he just challenge me? Because I love a good challenge, I think to myself.

"I'm in." I bang my fist on the couch like they do in the movies when they're about to begin the training montage. The *Rocky* theme song begins to play in my head.

"Okay, then the first step is for us to do some tests, and then you'll head to group therapy."

I smile, but try not to make it too big of a smile, even though this is the most hope I've had in, well, according to Dr. Anthony, four months.

That hope fades an hour later as I enter the room where group therapy is about to begin. These people *clearly* need to be here more than I do. What's more, an intense feeling that I should just get over what happened to me creeps into every pore of my body as I sit and listen to one patient after another explain what is happening with them.

Story after story of abuse, nearly dying from not eating enough, almost killing themselves with alcohol and drugs, permeates the room. And with each recounting, I grow less and less hopeful and feel more and more like I don't belong.

"Everyone, we have a new patient with us today. Nif, will you tell us why you're here?" the counselor leading the group says, breaking my thought spiral. I look around the room and fixate on this woman who is climbing distractingly on her chair. She sees me looking and hisses at me. I recoil as my hands snap in front of my face in a protective way. She is clearly crazy. Everyone breaks out into a sea of uncontrollable and somewhat nervous laughter as I fight back tears. It's jarring things like that that make my whole body tense up and intensify the never-ending pain I feel all over my skin.

The counselor shoots the woman a look of disapproval, and she sits back down in her chair, mumbling, "Sorry," as the counselor makes an encouraging gesture towards me.

"Go on, Nif."

"Well, I have PTSD…" I begin with a big gulp, my head turned down. The counselor asks me questions so that they can better understand. I look at them as if to beg them not to make me share in front of the room. I don't want to cry because I'll have to stay longer, but they won't let me off the hook and keep prodding. The rest of the patients grow, well, impatient, and I can feel their energy so intensely that I hesitantly share some of the details.

After I'm done describing some of the things that happened in the crash, I start to talk about the effects. The flashbacks, panic attacks, passing out, not sleeping, etc. I'm finally feeling okay with sharing when the woman who was up on her chair earlier interrupts with, "So what? You don't belong here. Just get over it. Clearly, you just want attention."

I can't hold back the tears and run out of the room, trying not to be seen by anyone. I run into one of the stalls in the bathroom and slink down to the floor. *She's right!* I think to myself. *See, everything you thought about yourself is true. Why can't you just get it together? You're such an idiot, and now everyone knows. Clearly,*

Dr. Anthony just gets money for keeping you here. You're going to be like this forever unless you can figure it out on your own. Why are you doing this? I sob and sob and sob until I'm too tired to cry anymore.

I walk to my room and lie on my bed and decide at that moment that I'm fine. I'm going to, as they say, fake it 'til I make it. And, even if I'm not fine, I'm going to pretend like hell that I am so I can get out of here. That woman was right. I don't belong here.

Just then, the counselor from the group comes to my room. "Nif, are you okay?"

"I'm fine." I keep myself turned toward the wall so he can't see just how not fine I actually am.

"Please don't take to heart what was said in the group. Everyone in there is struggling with their own issues, and you have every right to be here and get the help you need to get better and be happy."

Counselors talk so weird, I think to myself. *Every right? Like, why would anyone want to even have that right? I just want to go home.*

"I'm okay, really," I reply

"Okay, well, I'll see you in the next group session."

And then, he was gone. *NEXT GROUP SESSION?!* I think as panic starts to take over. How many of those are there going to be? I try to calm myself down as I lie there, scared, not knowing what to do. My efforts are in vain because, as much as I try, I can't control the flashbacks or panic attacks when they come, and a full-blown flashback ensues. I can hear my roommate yell for the nurses. *Crap, she's scared. I can hear it. I totally forgot to warn her. I suck so much.* Two nurses come into the room and give me a shot of something that knocks me right out. The sweet relief of sleep takes over my body.

Chapter Twenty-Three

THE SUN SHINES THROUGH THE WINDOW, HITTING ME right in the eyes as I wince from the brightness. I roll over, a bit groggy as the events of yesterday come flooding back to me. I roll away from the wall and see Claire lying on her bed reading a magazine. She looks at me, and I give her a half smile.

"Sorry about yesterday," I say, feeling more guilt than I care to admit. "I should have warned you about my flashbacks."

"Don't worry about it. I've been here several times. Nothing surprises me. Though I haven't ever seen what you went through. Are you okay?"

"Yeah, I'm fine. They happen to me all the time. I wish I could control them. I hate that they make everyone around me so… I don't know. I just wish they would stop." I also wish this conversation was over, but I am relieved that she doesn't seem to be traumatized by my trauma.

"Well, hang in there," she says in an encouraging tone.

"Ladies, it's time for group therapy." A nurse peeks her head in our doorway.

"Crap! I can't believe I slept so late." I jump out of bed and run to the bathroom before heading to the therapy room.

I guess being late was a slight blessing in disguise. I didn't have time to psych myself out of going or get worked up. I make my way to an empty chair and sit down, hoping the therapist won't call on me today.

Oh thank god, I think as I walk out of therapy and make my way back to my room. I am not asked to speak in group and am able to just sit and listen. It's a nice change.

"See, your problems aren't even worth asking about," the woman from the day before hisses at me as she bumps into me in the hall. I fight back tears. All I want to do is lie on my bed and curl up with the blanket my mom made for me. It has running horses on it, and it's so soft and cozy. I'm so grateful for it because it makes me feel safe.

I walk in and see that my bed has been made. The cleaning people are not supposed to do that. *It's so nice of them,* I am thinking when I notice that the horses are running upside down. I begin to feel panic. I know this is not normal. Like, who cares if the horses are running upside down? But I can't fight it. I absolutely need to fix this situation, immediately. I frantically tear the blanket off the bed. *Why are you freaking out, Nif? No one is dying here. It's just a blanket!* I am screaming to myself. But I can't stop. It feels like if I don't fix this, something horrible is going to happen. I start to panic as tears roll down my face. It's like I'm acting without any control over my body. I absolutely *have* to fix it. I find myself rubbing my hand over the soft fabric of the blanket over and over again like I'm petting one of those horses. As if to say, "There, there, now you're okay. It's going to be okay."

"Oh, got a little OCD, do ya?" Claire chuckles as she comes into the room.

"What?" I respond, wiping the tears away, hoping she won't notice. I have no idea what she's even talking about and kind of don't want to talk. But she takes my "what" as a prompt for conversation, and I'm just too tired to think of a way out of it.

"OCD. Obsessive Compulsive Disorder. So many people here have it. It's not a big deal… well, unless it is. It's basically where you do crazy things like pet your blanket, obsessively. I had a roommate once who would spend like 15 minutes every morning making sure all the yarn on her bunny slippers was facing the same way. You ask me, if I was her doctor, I would have taken those things away from her. It was nuts."

"Oh, um, I don't *think* I have that," I say, trying to not engage, but is she right? I've had so many conditions and acronyms thrown at me since the crash; this might have been one of them, and I just don't remember. God I wish my flipping brain would work again. I used to be sharp, smart, and clever. Now I'm just an idiot who can't remember basic words, stutters when she talks, and breaks down at the drop of a hat. I hate this.

My roommate is sharp, though, and can totally take a hint. She sees that I want to be alone and starts to head out the door.

"Do you want me to come get you for lunch?" she asks on her way out.

"Sure." I'm completely distracted by the possibility of having OCD. *What does that mean for my getting out of here? Is it another thing I'm going to have to fake that I'm better from? Because if it is, I don't know if I can. It really is hard to control, nearly impossible, in fact. Ugh.* I lie down and wrap myself in my blanket and try to think of something else.

Chapter Twenty-Four

"Hey, you coming to art therapy?" Claire asks as she whisks through our room like a tornado.

"Sure." I am grateful for the distraction, even though I have no idea what art therapy is. I typically like art, so I am happy to check it out. Also, anything to get me out of my head. It's been like two hours since Claire mentioned this OCD thing, and it's all I can think about. I've been sitting here trying not to panic about it. Like, what the heck am I going to do with this never-ending list of things I need to "heal" from? Can you even heal from this?

As we walk toward the room, I see a new face talking to one of the nurses at the nurse stand. She's a young woman, doesn't appear much older than me, if older at all. She seems really familiar with everyone and everything, and I think maybe I just missed her the last few days.

She sees me looking at her, says goodbye to the nurse she was talking to, and comes up to my roommate and me with a little skip and a chipper, "Hi, I'm Kaley." She stretches her hand out to shake mine. I do the same.

"I'm Nif," I say with way less enthusiasm. She seems like the most normal, happy person I've ever met. I can't understand why she'd be here.

We all walk together to the art therapy room. There are three other patients and a therapist. The room is open with shelves along all four walls full of art supplies and a large table in the middle with chairs all around it. I feel like I'm back in school. It's kind of comforting. There are a few pieces of paper in front of each of the chairs with little boxes of chalk laid out kitty-corner to the paper. I straighten mine so that the angle is even with the paper. My roommate sees me, mouths, "OCD," and nods toward the chalk box.

OH MY GOD! I think. I've been doing stuff like that without thinking about it for months now. What the heck?! I mean, I've always been sort of particular, so I didn't think anything of it, but now it's not just particular. It's a heavy action. Like, I can't stop myself from doing those things. This whole PTSD thing is so annoying. I mean, seriously. But, whatever, I'm excited to learn about the chalks because I've never worked with chalk as a medium before, so I turn my attention back to the therapist as she explains what we're going to do.

"There's this concept laid out in this book called *Drawing on the Right Side of the Brain* that we're going to explore today. The idea is that if you don't know what object you're drawing, you can turn the analytical part of your brain off and actually draw the object. So, you'll find a photo covered by a piece of paper in front of you. Take the paper and expose only the bottom two inches of the picture and, without trying to figure out what the picture is, draw what you see."

Huh? I think, and almost as if she heard my thoughts, the therapist says, "Just trust me. It's going to be fun. Trust the process."

Trust, trust, trust, I think as I go about choosing the color of chalk I want to use. I pick a deep, dark red color. The chalk feels cool to the touch, and I love that my fingers already look like artist's fingers, full of color. I place the chalk on the paper and draw only what I see. Each time I finish the two inches that are exposed, I expose two more inches and two more until the entire picture is exposed, and I am done drawing. *Holy crap! It worked.* I have drawn a bowl of fruit, and it looks like an actual bowl of fruit. I've never been able to draw anything resembling a real thing in my life. This is so cool. All I want to do is do more of this.

"Okay, how did everyone do?" the therapist asks, and we begin going around the table talking about how the exercise made us feel. Art therapy is super cool, and I wish I could just do this every minute of the day moving forward.

"I love drawing with chalk," Kaley chimes in as the therapist tells us we can spend the rest of the time doing whatever we want.

"Yeah, I've never used it before, and I kind of love it too," I respond.

"What brings you here?" Kaley asks in a way no one has asked before. She's super non-judgmental and just has this light and breezy energy no one else in this place does. I'm digging it.

I tell her about my PTSD and then ask her what she's here for, and she responds, "Oh, a reset." I look at her, super confused, and she laughs. "Sorry, I forget that not everyone has my sense of humor about mental illness."

I say, "I want to, though."

She chuckles. "I have bipolar disorder, and about twice a year, I check myself in here to regulate my medications and sort of… well, reset. I used to feel really embarrassed about my mental illness, but now, I just think of it like anything else. It's something I have, it makes me who I am, and when I start to feel off, I know exactly what I need to do to get back on track. That includes checking myself in here. Some of the medications I'm on are really powerful, so if I try to regulate on my own, it can be dangerous." She looks at me and sees the confusion on my face and continues, "It's like… hmmm… have you ever gone a whole day without eating, and your body doesn't feel good, and you get super crabby?" I nod. "But then you eat something and you miraculously feel better." She waits for me to respond. I nod again. "It's like that only, obviously, a bit more extreme. I've just come to recognize through years with this diagnosis when my body isn't quite right and I need a metaphorical sandwich." She laughs at the silliness of the analogy, and I laugh along with her but at the same time am fascinated by what she's saying.

We do a little more art and have probably the best time I've had in months, all while I'm thinking about her perspective. She's so open and explains what it's like to have bipolar disorder and some of the tools she uses to keep her spirits up and keep her wits about her as she navigates something that sounds really difficult.

She holds up her chalk drawing of Dory from *Finding Nemo* and states with the utmost confidence, "This is definitely one of the ways I keep my spirits up."

"I don't understand."

"It's Dory from *Finding Nemo.*" She looks at me, confused, and I can tell that she's wondering what I don't understand.

"I get that. But how does Dory help you keep your spirits up?"

"Well, if I'm feeling sad or discouraged by what's happening in my mind, I just sing her song to remind myself to just keep swimming, swimming, swimming," she sings with a big smile on her face as she writes the words at the top of her chalk drawing of Dory.

I begin to sing along, and we both laugh and head out to put the picture up on the wall.

"I like to hang positive things up on the walls. It can get so dark in all our heads, ya know? I've found that when things are really dark inside, it helps to surround yourself with light, positive things on the outside." She explains her perspective while she hangs the picture up with individual pieces of tape she got from the nurse's station. They wouldn't let us have the actual dispenser because of the sharp edges. Being in the psych ward is wild.

Chapter Twenty-Five

THE NEXT DAY, FEELING INSPIRED BY WHAT KALEY HAD to say about surrounding yourself with positive things, I head to the art therapy room. I remember there are old magazines there that I could use for a project I wanted to do. I was right! I grab the magazines and walk as quickly as I can to the nurse's station. I haven't had this much hope and energy since the crash. Kaley is a lifesaver. She had to go to individual therapy, or I'd have asked her to join me.

At the nurse's station, I am relieved to see that it's one of the nice nurses. There are some that just aren't cool at all. They make life real difficult. *My luck is taking a turn for the better. First I get to do art therapy, then I get to know Kaley, and now a good nurse is at the station. Maybe this will all work out after all.*

"Is it okay if I sort of destroy these magazines?" I ask. The nurse looks at me, confused, so I explain. "I'd like to do an art project."

"Oh," he replies. "Sure."

"Cool, do you have posterboard?"

"Yep," he responds

"Great, do you have glue?"

"Yep," he says, once again.

"Awesome!" This is going really well. When I was a kid, I used to take my mom's fashion magazines and cut out pictures of the women I wanted to be like, the places I wanted to see, or clothes I wanted to wear, and I'd put them up on the wall. It was a way to surround myself with life outside of dreaded Karlville. These women in the pictures were living the way I wanted to live, and it inspired me so much. I'm so excited to create this right now!

"Do you have scissors?" I ask, completely caught up in the moment and the excitement.

The nurse, who was also caught up in my excited energy, pauses with the word "yep" halfway out of his mouth so it sort of sounds like, "Yeeeennnnoooo." We both look at each other and realize what I had just asked for. "Yeah, no." He looks at me like, duh, you should know patients aren't allowed to have sharp objects.

I look around and remember where I am. Of course we're not. But how am I going to make my collage without scissors? I feel defeated, but also determined, so I take what I can get and walk back to the art therapy room.

I lay out the magazines, the posterboard, and the glue on the table in front of me. I am feeling better than I have in longer than I can remember, but my brain still isn't working as well as it used to. I open the magazines and start flipping through. "How am I going to do this without scissors?" I think to myself, and then Zane's voice shoots into my head like a laser. *When what you want seems impossible, you have to focus on it even more. Aggressive optimism. Hello, you just saw it in action with Kaley. How can you make this collage? I mean, right now, at least you can get started on finding the pictures you'd like to have on your collage.*

I find a picture of this young girl laughing—full out. The joy radiating from her is palpable. Without even thinking about it, I rip the page out of the magazine. *Wait!* I think. I don't need scissors. I can just rip around the pictures I want to put on my collage. I feel relieved and joyful. *It's already working. Thanks, Nana*, I think to myself with a smile.

For the next couple of hours, I flip and rip and flip and rip all sorts of images out of the magazines. It definitely takes longer to rip around the pictures than it does to cut them, but, I must admit, it's also a bit more cathartic. It gives me time to focus on my intention, as Zane's grandma is always pointing out. "If we want anything in this world, we must pursue it with intention." And the ripping sound just makes it feel more… I don't know the word… just more. I am liking this happy accident.

With all the pictures ripped out, I arrange and glue them onto the posterboard. I hold the collage up and realize that, unlike the collages I used to make when I was a kid, this collage is all about how I want to feel. There are peaceful images of nature, one in particular of a woman holding a bunch of orange blossoms. I can almost smell the sweet scent through the picture, and it calms my mind. There is one of a child riding the teacups at Disneyland, and I can almost hear the belly laugh she must have had. There's one of the sky where the clouds spell out "dream," and I'm taken back to when I was a kid and my family and I would go to the park and look up at the sky and try to find shapes in the clouds. Looking at this brings a huge smile to my face.

These are all images of feelings that I haven't had in my life since that old man ran us all over, essentially knocking the joy right out of my body. I want to dream about these images when I close my eyes, not the images of dead people and blood that have been haunting me for four months. I want to be able to laugh instead of having a flashback if someone silly scares me for fun. I want my life to be what it was before that day. And, for the first time since the crash, I am actually feeling these emotions, looking at the collage I just made. And along with the emotions comes a tiny glimmer of hope.

I begin to sob, quietly, alone in that room. Big, giant, whole-body sobbing.

"Nif, are you okay?" Kaley's voice breaks through the silent sobs as she comes to sit next to me.

"I'm good." I wipe away the tears. "I'm actually really good. I was inspired by what you said about surrounding yourself with positive images, and I made this." I hold up my collage, and Kaley squeals and claps.

"That is so cool!" Her smile grows bigger as she looks over all the images in detail. I've noticed she is a very careful and thoughtful person, so she would never just glance at something. I can tell as she takes in each image that she is considering how it might apply to me and her and life and everyone.

"I love it. Let's go hang it up." She grabs the collage, and we walk to my room.

Chapter Twenty-Six

I LET OUT A SIGH, LOOKING AT THE COLLAGE FROM yesterday. It is the perfect way to remind myself of the feelings I want to have back in my life. I smile. The sun is shining in through the window as I put on my slippers and grab my stuff to head to the shower. It's been a whole week since I checked into this place, and I have slept through the night every night since I got here. I notice how good I'm feeling as I walk past my still-sleeping roommate. She gets to go home today and has been packing since she got the news yesterday. I'm happy for her and am also going to miss her. I hope I get the same news this afternoon when I have my appointment with Dr. Anthony.

The water feels good on my skin as I take note that it's the first time in months that water running onto my skin doesn't feel like a really bad sunburn. Maybe I really am getting better. It doesn't seem possible, so I shift my focus to the smell of the body wash my parents brought me when they came to visit yesterday. It smells like strawberries, and it brings me back to the summers I used to spend with my grandma picking strawberries from her garden and then making strawberry sundaes. My grandma was the best.

I showed them my collage, but all it seemed to do was make them sad. I am super torn about having them visit because I can see how worried they are about me, and I feel so much pressure to just be better. But whenever I try to explain what's going on, they don't understand, which gets really frustrating. I wish I could say it isn't upsetting, but yesterday, after they left, I had to take extra sleeping medicine because my body just wouldn't calm down. It's so annoying. I am totally feeling better emotionally ever since Kaley and I had our conversation, but it doesn't seem to translate into how my body is doing. Sometimes, it's like my mind and body are fighting against each other. The good thing is, now that I'm sleeping, the fight isn't as exhausting as it used to be, so I'm still feeling hopeful.

Once I'm ready, I head to the art therapy room. This is definitely my favorite place on the floor, and I especially like it because Kaley is almost always there too. Today it is a popular place. Kaley's there along with Mira, who has an eating disorder, Tim, who is an addict, and Bill, who has severe depression. My roommate is also there, saying goodbye to everyone before her boyfriend comes to pick her up.

Everyone is doing their own projects and chatting away when Rosa, a woman in her forties, comes in and strips down to her underwear, yelling, "I'm free! I'm free!" The nurses come running in and give her some medicine to calm her down as they take her back to her room.

Rosa also has bipolar disorder like Kaley, but clearly doesn't have the same type of family support that Kaley has because Tim leans over and whispers, "Her husband is coming to take her home today."

"What?!" I respond, feeling super upset. "She clearly needs to be here. Why doesn't her family see that?"

Kaley puts her hand on my arm as a way of comforting me and calming me down. "Mental illness is really hard for a lot of people to understand, let alone accept. It's, like, you can see a broken bone so you can believe it and then feel confident about treating it. You can't see a broken mind, so lots of people just deny its existence. I think that's what Rosa's husband is doing, and since Rosa isn't technically a harm to herself or anyone else, the hospital can't keep her. It's really sad."

I'm so upset at this realization. "It's more than sad. It should be illegal. Rosa has been doing so good. What happened?"

No one knows, nor do they seem to care. Everyone just goes back to their art projects. I can't just sit here and do nothing, so I go to Rosa's room to see if I can help.

An orderly is standing outside of Rosa's room and puts his arm across the door as I try to enter.

"Nif, you can't go in there."

"But I just want to help. Rosa needs help. Why is this happening? She just needs help!" I start to get worked up. "It's not fair that no one is helping her!"

He turns me away, and I feel so helpless. I hate that feeling. I just don't understand how someone could just let their loved one suffer because they don't want to accept that they're sick. I mean, if Rosa had cancer, would her husband deny it and not let her get chemotherapy? I gather myself and head back to the art therapy room.

Everyone is still chatting away. Mira is talking about how her modeling agent doesn't want her in here much longer because she might gain weight. I lean in and try to encourage her. "Mira, maybe you should look into acting instead of modeling. Modeling is clearly not good for you if the people around you *want* you to have an eating disorder."

I pick up the drawing that I was working on and go to put it on the shelf so Kaley and I can hang it up later. It's kind of become our thing to decorate the halls with happy pictures. As I am walking over to the shelf, I overhear Bill comment on a dark thought that has been permeating his mind lately. Instead of putting the drawing on the shelf, I decide to give it to Bill. "Bill, I made this for you. Hopefully, it will help you replace the dark thoughts with something positive. I know that's not always easy, but I've noticed that I am feeling better now that I've started to surround myself with positive images." Bill takes the drawing and gives me a hug as thanks. It feels really good to be able to make someone else feel better.

As I walk back to my seat, I hear Tim confiding in my roommate. "I wish I were ready to go home, but I don't think I'm strong enough to deal with my job and coworkers yet."

I ask, "Why not, Tim? You seem to be doing fine here."

My roommate interjects, "Nif, I know you're just trying to help, but you don't know anything about addiction. It's not as simple out there as it is in here." I feel embarrassed, but know she's right. I don't know how to respond, so I just lower my head and walk away, trying to hide my face because I know how red it must be.

"Nif, it's time for your appointment with Dr. Anthony," the nurse says from the door. I'm so grateful to have an excuse to get out of there. And I'm really excited for my appointment because I think I'm doing so much better. I mean, I've slept every night. Sure, I needed extra medicine last night, but that should be fine. I've been in much better spirits. I've been helping Kaley decorate the walls. I've been trying to help the other patients as much as I can. I think I'm making real progress.

"Hi, Nif." Dr Anthony looks up from his notebook as I walk into his office.

"Hi." I take a seat on his oversized couch. I really hate this couch. It's so big that I feel like I can't get myself situated. I move around for a couple minutes trying to get comfortable and then give up and deal with the fact that I'm going to go through this entire appointment with my right butt cheek being slightly higher than my left while leaning on my hand to make sure I don't tip over. Who the heck designed this thing anyway? I'm convinced they were definitely at least six feet tall.

Anyway, focus, I think to myself as I turn my attention to Dr. Anthony.

"How are you feeling?" he asks, as he always does.

"Fine." I notice he's not smiling. "Good, I mean, great. I'm doing great." I'm really trying to get him to see that I'm good enough to go home, just like I do every day. The thing is that today should be different for all the reasons I stated above. I'm like a model patient. If there were grades for patienting, I would certainly get an A.

But my hope is slowly dissipating as Dr. Anthony looks at me the way he looks at me every day. With the "Are you sure?" look. *YES I'M SURE!* is what I want to yell, but yelling random things out loud is a sure sign you are crazy.

"Nif, some of the nurses have noticed that you are spending a lot of time giving advice to other patients."

"I know! Isn't it great? I'm starting to feel like my old self," I say cheerfully, and then I look at him, and he's not smiling. In fact, he's looking at me with disappointment.

"Nif, we've talked about this. There's a reason you are here, and it is not to help the other patients. It's to help yourself. Now, do you think that focusing on other people's issues is going to help you heal your own?" he asks and then sits there waiting for me to respond.

"I'm so confused. I mean, I haven't felt this good in months. How can what I'm doing be bad? I'm just trying to help them," I plead, hoping to convince him that he's wrong in his assessment of the situation.

"I know you see it that way, but two things... one, you are not a doctor, and therefore, the advice you give might actually harm the person you're giving it to if you don't know their whole situation. And, two, and probably the most important, if you don't learn how to deal with your own issues in here, then most likely, they'll be impossible to deal with out there." He points out the window. "And then you'll end up right back where you started. Do you want that to happen?"

I absolutely do not want that to happen, so I ask, "What do I have to do?"

"Well, I've noticed you haven't been writing in your journal. I know you said that you weren't able to get the words from your brain to the page when you first came to us, but do you think you've gotten to a point where you might be able to write? I've noticed your stutter has stopped, so maybe you can give writing a try again. What do you think?"

Don't freak out, I order myself. I have really come to hate trying to write since the crash. It makes me feel like an idiot. All I do is write the same three words over and over again. It's the same with reading. It's like my brain gets stuck and just keeps skipping like a broken record. But, if journaling is what I need to do to prove to Dr. Anthony that I'm better and can go home, I'm willing to try. "I can try."

A smile appears across his face. "Great! If you can get through a couple days of journaling and learn to focus on yourself, I think we can assess you going home."

His words bring a smile to my face.

I skip to the phone and call my parents and tell them about my appointment with Dr. Anthony.

They sound relieved.
I smile as I hang up the phone.

Chapter Twenty-Seven

I turn over in bed to see that there's someone new sleeping in my roommate's bed. She must have come in during the night. *Wow, these sleep meds are powerful. I used to wake up at the sound of a squeak in the floor,* I think to myself. *Remember what it was like for you when you came in during the night. Be extra nice to this woman,* I tell myself as I slide my feet into my slippers, trying not to wake her.

They must have given her some powerful sleeping medication too because she doesn't even move as I walk by to head to the bathroom. When I get back, she's still sleeping, but I don't want to wait for her to wake up before I start my day. Today is visitor's day, which is different from when my parents come to visit. Today, anyone—family, friends—can come and visit, and I get to see Zane and Karsten. I'm so excited I could… aaahhh, there are no words to describe how excited I am. I haven't seen them in over a week, and the only phone calls I'm allowed are to my family. I tried to explain that they are family, but it's only legal family. So annoying.

Anyway, I've made both of them chalk drawings and want to head to the art therapy room to make sure that they are ready before heading into group therapy. So I leave a note on my new roommate's nightstand in the hopes that she'll see it when she wakes up and won't feel as scared as I did.

It definitely takes longer to write than it would have before the crash, but it doesn't take as long as it would have taken when I first got to the hospital. In fact, when I first arrived, I wouldn't have been able to finish. But I work my way through a few skips and am able to write a little paragraph.

Good morning! My name is Nif and I'm your roommate. Just wanted you to know this place isn't as scary as it seems. See you when you wake up. ☺

I lay it next to the lamp on her bedside table and smile.

Finally! It's two o'clock. I rush out of group therapy and to the common area where we get to meet our friends and family. I see Zane and Karsten and almost run another patient over trying to get to them.

"Sorry." I rush by and run to be embraced by my two best friends. It feels so familiar and safe as I smell the sweet lavender of Zane's shampoo. I don't want to let go. We embrace and break long enough to scream and jump around, and then we embrace again. It lasts about three minutes, at which time we calm ourselves down and head to my room.

Sitting on my bed, Zane and Karsten fill me in on all the drama happening at Karlville High.

"Honestly, sweetie, I don't think Jessa knows what to do without you. It's like for the past four years, her life has revolved around this little made-up feud of hers, and now that you're not there, she is beside herself trying to find her place in the world. She literally asked how you were the other day. It was creepy," Karsten said in his familiar, flamboyant, overly dramatic tone.

Ugh, I missed him. I can't lie. I smile as he tells me the stories of Jessa being so lost. Serves her right.

"Yeah, and Mrs. M says to tell you hello and that she hopes you get to come back to school soon. She really misses you. Everyone does. I mean, clearly, even Jessa. You're such an important part of the fabric of Karlville," Zane adds. Both Karsten and I look at her like *what?* And the three of us bust out laughing. "Okay, maybe that was a bit of a stretch, but I just want you to know how loved you are and how missed you are." Zane tries to explain why she went a little off the edge just then.

The two of them continue with story after story, talking over each other and laughing while I sit and watch, engulfed in their energy. But knowing I'm not at their level yet. I still don't have it in me to engage in that way, and I begin to question whether or not I ever will again. The thing is, being here, having gone through all that I've gone through, has made me realize how trivial high school can be, and I'm not sure if I'll ever find the level of care I used to have for that kind of thing again. It's really hard to care what Jessa thinks of me after hearing about how Tim almost overdosed in the room next to his newborn while he was taking care of him. Or how Kaley's manic episodes have cost her family so much money due to her extreme shopping that they've almost lost their house. Or how Mira literally starved herself to the point of having to be put on life support.

These are real dramas, not whether I'm going to ace my history test or even get the solo in the spring concert. I begin to feel sad at this revelation. I wish I could go back to caring about "normal" high school things. But I just don't see that happening. That said, I know I will never not love these two goofballs in front of me chatting away, and so I practice the tool of being present and join in the conversation by blurting out, "I just love you two."

My outburst is met with a collective "Aaaawwwweeee" and another group hug.

"Oh, we made you something," Zane says, breaking our group hug.

"Ohhhh, I love presents." I clap my hands with glee.

Zane grabs her oversized, Hawaiian-print bag and pulls out a beautiful yellow journal.

Holding the journal close to her chest, she begins to speak as if she's reading off a grocery list. "Your mom told us that one of your therapies was to journal. She also told us that you are *not* enjoying it. She also told us that you are working on surrounding yourself with things that are positive and make you happy. So, do you remember the phrase my grandma came up with, the one I shared with you at the homecoming concert? Aggressive optimism?"

"Yeah, of course I do. I love that phrase, and I love the concept. I can't believe I had forgotten about it. I actually remembered it just the other day when I was doing the collage. It helped me so much. I can't believe we're so on the same page," I say as I gesture that we have the same mind.

"I'm so happy to hear you say that!" Zane says in her most proper way as Karsten claps in his most dramatic way.

Karsten bites his scarf in gleeful anticipation as Zane ceremoniously hands me the journal that is embossed with the phrase AGGRESSIVE OPTIMISM. I can't believe what I'm seeing as I take the journal and hold it to my chest. A few moments pass as I try to find the words to express how much this means to me. All I can come up with is, "Thank you."

But, looking at their faces, I can see that they don't need me to say anything else. We all start tearing up, and Karsten breaks the silence by inviting us into a group hug.

Chapter Twenty-Eight

"Hey, Nif, you okay?" Kaley asks from the doorway. "It's pretty late. I've already had breakfast."

"Oh, I guess I didn't get much sleep last night. I'm feeling a little anxious," I say, getting up in my bed.

"You should definitely tell the nurses so they can make sure the medication you're on is still working," she advises.

"Yeah, nothing like being a chemistry experiment to start the day off right," I chuckle because after being here for over a week, I'm starting to feel okay talking about medication. I mean, before I came here, I must have tried fifteen different kinds. Most didn't work at all, some made me a zombie, some made me more hyper than if I ate twenty Pixy Stix, and one, the scariest reaction of all so far, left me unable to move. I remember waking up looking around and realizing I could not move my body at all. I was trapped in my bed. It was in the middle of the night, and the only person home was Jane, so I just lay there, shut my eyes, and tried to calm my breathing. I slept it off and was fine the next day, but it was something I'll never forget. Being a science experiment, something Kaley and I jokingly call ourselves, in the hospital is a lot better than doing it on my own at home. But I still feel a lot of shame around medication. Needing it at all makes me feel like a weakling. But I just keep reminding myself that it is helping me heal.

I walk out to the nurse's station and hesitantly tell them what's going on, trying not to be a bother or make a bigger deal out of it than it is. That goal is trashed when they immediately call Dr. Anthony in the most urgent tone. He advises them on a new medication to give me. They rush to grab it like I'm in cardiac arrest or something. Sometimes their urgency makes me feel like such a burden. I take the tiny pill and have a seat on the chairs near the nurse's station per protocol. They need to monitor me to make sure I don't have a reaction to the medication. This is nothing new. I've had to do this about ten times since I got here. Nothing major has happened, which is nice. I'm grateful to have them here in case I have some of the reactions I had at home, but other than being paralyzed, I haven't had any serious reactions. With that said, I've seen some. Holy cow! There was one guy who took a new medication, sitting in the chair I'm sitting in now, and I walked by just as his face swelled up so much that his eyes were just slivers between puffy cheeks and eyebrows. His face was as red as an apple. Thanks goodness the nurses noticed immediately and shot him with an EpiPen. He's fine now, and I see him around every once in a while. Not often because he usually hangs out in the TV room, which is still not a place I go. A shiver runs down my spine just thinking about it.

I shift in my seat a little and start to feel super strange. My heart starts pumping; my skin starts to feel like it isn't my own, like it's crawling and all I want to do is rip it off. I begin tearing at the magazine sitting on the chair next to the one I'm sitting in. *It's fine,* I think to myself. I mean, as far as I can tell, my face is still normal, so no allergic reaction, right? *So, why do I feel this way? This isn't normal.* I don't know what to do, so I begin pacing in front of the nurse's station. They should notice if I'm up out of my seat pacing, right? I mean, they are supposed to be monitoring me, right?

Nope. Nope, they don't. Oh god, what should I do? I don't know how to handle this situation. I don't know the words to use to get them to see me or understand. It feels super strange, and I can't tell if it's all in my head or if it's going to stop soon, so I just keep pacing. Back and forth, back and forth for what seems like forever.

Is this really happening? What even is *this?* I've never experienced anything like this before.

I know. I'll grab the magazine I was ripping up and do it in front of them. Yeah, that'll work. If they see me ripping at magazines, they'll have to notice that something is wrong, and I need to do something to get this energy out of me. Rip, rip, rip, pace, pace, pace. Nothing. *How do I get their attention without being over the top? They're clearly busy since none of them have noticed all this is happening. I don't want to interrupt them.*

What should I do? I can't believe this is happening. I don't want to live like this anymore. I'm tired of feeling like a pinball in a machine getting smacked around. One minute, I'm up, and the next, I'm down. Up, down, up, down. I can't take it anymore. I just want to die.

I make my way to the kitchen. No one is in there. Thank god because I don't want to bug anyone with this. I rummage through the drawers. Nothing sharp. Of course, it's a psych ward. They don't even let you have shoelaces.

This'll do. I begin to saw at my wrist with a plastic knife. Just sawing, sawing, sawing, not really able to see through the haze that this medication is creating not only in my brain, but also in my eyes. Kaley comes in. "NIF! WHAT ARE YOU DOING?! GIVE ME THE KNIFE!"

"NO! I CAN'T TAKE IT ANYMORE!" I run out of the cafeteria with the knife still sawing at my wrist. I run into my room and try to hide in the corner by the bed, but the orderlies find me, and I feel a pinch in my neck and then blackness.

My eyes are heavy as I blink them awake. It takes a minute, but then I realize I'm lying in a bed. I try to move, only to find that my hands and feet are in straps attached to the bed. The room I'm in is unlike any room I've ever seen before, but I recognize the style from TV. *A padded room?! Really? They exist?*

"Why am I here?" I yell. "Hello? Is anyone there?"

Dr. Anthony and a nurse walk in. "Nif, do you know what happened?" Dr. Anthony asks.

"No. What happened? Why am I strapped to this bed, and what happened to my arm?" I respond, looking at my left wrist wrapped in gauze.

Dr. Anthony explains what had happened just a few hours earlier after I went to the kitchen, and it all comes flooding back. I explain to him what had happened before I went to the kitchen and how no one even looked up from the desk as I was trying to get their attention.

"Why didn't you just ask for help?" Dr. Anthony asks.

"I didn't want to bug them," I respond.

He looks at me with a sense of realization that quickly turns to sadness.

I can't handle it when he looks at me this way, so I turn away and try to bury my head in the pillow and cry.

Chapter Twenty-Nine

"WHERE THE HECK AM I?" I THINK AS I STIR AWAKE and look around this unfamiliar room. It looks pretty much the same as my other room, except it has its own bathroom, the furniture is flipped, and there are video cameras mounted in each corner of the room. A chill comes over me, and I grab the horse blanket without thinking about it. I pause with the realization that all my stuff is here. *Okay, so, I'm not in the padded room anymore. That's good, but, wow, I must have been out because I don't remember getting moved here, and it was daytime when Dr. Anthony and I talked about what had happened. Now it's pitch-black outside. Okay, don't freak out. Why are there cameras everywhere? Why does this room have its own bathroom? What is going on? Breathe, breathe, breathe.* I'm about to have a panic attack when the door opens, and a nurse walks in.

"Hi, Nif, you're in the monitoring room now," the nurse says matter-of-factly, like I'm supposed to know what that means. *What the heck is the monitoring room?* "How are you feeling?"

"Like I'm in prison. What is the monitoring room?"

"Well, it's where we put people who are on suicide watch." She puts the cuff on to check my blood pressure.

"Suicide watch? I'm not suicidal. It was a reaction to the medication."

"Whatever it was, you sawed at your wrist. Actually drew blood, which can't be easy with a plastic knife, so, suicide watch it is. You'll be staying here until Dr. Anthony clears you to move back to a regular room. Let me know if you need anything."

"I need to get out of here so I can go home in a couple days," I reply.

"Oh, sweetie, that's not going to happen anytime soon, not after what happened today." She exits the room.

She leaves me there alone in this cold, sterile room. I lie on the bed knowing I've ruined everything, and her attitude about it just makes it worse. I look around and see that they've brought the pictures from the wall of my room and laid them on a small table. I grab the pictures and begin to tear them up. *I can't believe this is happening. I've been working so hard. It wasn't my fault. The medication did this to me, and none of the stupid nurses noticed. Why am I being punished for something that was out of my control? I HATE THIS PLACE! I HATE MY BRAIN! I HATE MYSELF! You know what, I do want to die! It would be such a relief to end all of this.* I slink to the ground, drop my head into my knees, and sob. It feels like all that I've gone through to get better in the hospital never happened and that I'm right back where I started. I fall asleep on the hard, cold floor.

A few hours later, I wake up with a cramp in my neck. Dried tears mixed with dirt from the floor coat my face. It's gross. I get up from the floor and sit on the bed. I go to turn the light out when I see the journal Zane and Karsten made for me sitting there, just staring at me, begging me to open it. I do, and I see messages from the two of them that I hadn't seen when they gave it to me. They read:

Dear Nif,

First of all, you are stronger than anyone openly gives you credit for. I know you think I don't notice, but I do. I am grateful you exist in this world and that we get to be friends. Please hang in there so we can have more sleepovers and gossip about all the things that don't matter because it's fun.

Love, the Queen,
Karsten

Nif,

My sister from another mister. You are such a light in this world. Please know that you are loved and that the world is better because you're in it. I know things are dark right now, but, as my nana would say to me when I was sad, let me be your light until you can find your own again.

Love & Light,

Zane

I run my finger over their words as if to absorb them through my skin. Then, as if the words are actual electricity, I feel a jolt. I suddenly know exactly what to do. I open up the book, grab the super short pencil—because they won't give me anything that might allow me to hurt myself—and I begin to write out my plan. My plan for actually getting better so I can get out of here for real. No more faking it. I'm going to put in the work because my friends are holding out hope, and I'll be damned if I disappoint them, again.

My hand begins to cramp up from writing with such a short pencil, but I don't care. I get my plan down, put the journal back on the table, run my finger over the words AGGRESSIVE OPTIMISM, and fall asleep with a slight smile on my face. Tomorrow is another day, and I will face this issue head-on.

Chapter Thirty

I POP OUT OF BED WITH A DETERMINATION I HAVEN'T had in a long while. It's been two days since the *incident,* as I'm calling it, my ninth day in this place. It snowed last night, and as I look out the window at the fresh blanket of white fluff, I feel a sense of peace rush over me. I've never liked winters in Minnesota, but there really is nothing like the quiet a fresh blanket of snow can bring. And, even though I can't go outside or open my window, seventeen years of winters has created a visceral reaction to these types of mornings. I take a breath and just stand there breathing in the peace. I've been running the plan I wrote in my journal that night before last over and over in my head. I'm going to present my plan to Dr. Anthony today and am grateful that my appointment is early today, and it happens to be during group therapy time, bonus! Yeah, I still really don't like group therapy. But I look at it like vegetables. You gotta eat them if you want to be healthy.

"You got this," I sternly tell my reflection in the mirror as I brush my teeth.

"Hi, Dr. Anthony," I say as I sit on his uncomfortable couch. I don't even try and get comfortable today. I'm here to take care of business. I have my journal in hand but don't really need it as I've memorized the plan by now.

"Hi, Nif, how are you today?" he asks with a knowing smirk on his face. I think he knows how I am.

"Determined." I sit up as straight as I can and look him right in the eyes.

"I can see that. Then, why don't you go first?" He gestures for me to begin.

"Okay." I clear my throat and launch into telling him the plan. "I've taken what you said to heart. The part about taking care of myself. After the incident the other day where I didn't know how to ask for help when I desperately needed it, I've done a lot of reflection, and I've come to the conclusion that in order for me to really be able to focus on myself and begin to truly heal, I need to lock myself away for a bit. I just get so distracted by other people.

"I know that there is an empty room as of this morning, and I'd like to ask that I have it on my own so that I'm not distracted by other people's problems. I want to sit by myself and do the hard work of reflecting and journaling." I pause to see if he's still with me. He is, so I continue. "Along with that, I'd like to propose that I stay out of group therapy for the time being. When I'm there, I tend to compare my problems with everyone else's, and mine always seem minor in comparison." I look up; he's still with me. "Okay, then I'd like to propose actual journaling assignments. I do much better when I have things to focus on. You've said in the past that I won't have to deal with PTSD symptoms in the future as long as I process through the trauma. Sometimes, I don't know how to do that on my own, so I'd love it if you could give me journal prompts. What do you think?"

Dr. Anthony takes a long while before answering. He really is a thoughtful person, and I respect that even though, right now, all I want to do is yell, "WHAT DO YOU THINK?" But I stay calm, and he finally begins to talk. "Wow, Nif, you've really put some thought into this. I appreciate that, and I think we can make this plan happen." I let out a little yelp as he puts his hand up to calm me down as he continues. "That said, this is a pretty lofty plan, so I don't want you to think that you've failed if you can't achieve all of your goals right away. Are you willing to be honest with me if this starts to happen?"

"I hear what you are saying and agree that I tend to set myself up for failure because I remember all that I was able to accomplish before the crash. So, yes, I agree to keep you posted if I start to feel like I'm failing. As long as you agree to keep me honest if you notice I'm doing it and I am in denial. Deal?" I ask.

"Deal."

"Great!" I dive into the details.

"Oh," Dr. Anthony interrupts, "how is your reading coming along?"

"It's improved. I'm still not 100 percent, but I'm definitely getting stuck less and less. I think it's the fact that I'm sleeping."

"That makes total sense. The reason I ask is because there's a workbook with writing prompts that I can give you instead of making them up on my own." He walks across the room to his bookshelf, scanning the shelves for the workbook. "Oh, here it is." He walks back and hands me the workbook. I read *Writing Through Trauma* on the cover and feel a sense of hope.

Once the plan is solidified, we leave the room. Dr. Anthony walks over to the nurse's station to tell them I'll be moving into the empty room across the hall. They nod, and one of the nurses walks toward me. "Let's get your stuff!" I nod in agreement, and we head off to the monitoring room.

"I'm so glad to be leaving this room," I say as I pack my things up.

"I bet. This room doesn't look like it's any fun to be in." He fidgets because he's just standing there with nothing to do but watch me pack up. *This is awkward.*

We walk to the room that is going to be my saving grace. I can just feel things shifting already. I don't realize how great this new room is until I walk in. There's only one bed, so no risk of a new patient coming in while I'm asleep. The walls are a light yellow color, which is my favorite color, so I see it as a sign. I walk around taking in the bright, airy feel when I walk to the big window at the opposite end of the room and see the view, and I am immediately taken aback. It's a breathtaking view of a lake surrounded by pine trees and the fresh blanket of snow from last night. We are on the seventh floor so the view is endless. I watch as a mallard duck skims the water and a flock of geese flies overhead. The wind blows the tree branches lightly, and the sun hits my face, creating a warm sensation on my cheeks.

"Can I have some tape?" I ask, catching the nurse just as he was walking out the door. "I'd like to hang up my collage and make this room a cozy and inspiring space."

He nods, and we walk out to the nurse's station together. I'm smiling ear to ear.

Chapter Thirty-One

There, I think, running my hand over the blanket my mom made me. I step back to scan the room. I had spent the whole afternoon putting up pictures of people who inspire me, hanging my collage in the most prominent spot in the room, and making the bed so that the entire room felt cozy and inspiring. *Mission accomplished,* I think. Huh, and I didn't even obsess about whether the pictures were perfectly straight or if the blanket was perfectly placed on the bed. Though I did make sure the horses were running right side up. I mean, who in their right mind would be okay with horses running upside down?

I finish just in time for dinner and am putting my journal just right on the nightstand when Kaley pops her head in. "Hey, Nif, wanna go to dinner?" She looks around and comes all the way in. "Heeeeyyyyy, nice digs. This place looks great!"

"Thanks. I'm super happy with it. I'm just so glad that Dr. Anthony was on board with my plan for healing. Thanks for helping me tweak it. Your insight into being in the looney bin is quite valuable." I giggle. We both have a really flippant way of talking about mental illness because if we take our illness too seriously, we get worse. We were in group therapy the other day, and I said to the therapist, "I am broken."

And he got really upset and said, "I don't work with broken people. I work with people who are struggling." It made me feel like I couldn't explain to him how I felt, and I immediately shut down. Kaley came up to me afterward, and we had a long talk and came to the conclusion that his response was not helpful for people like us. We need to be able to express how we feel without being corrected. After that conversation, we decided that with each other, we would be the opposite of sensitive. We would be, frankly, kind of rude about how we talk about our mental illness. Look, we are crazy. That's just the reality. Will we be crazy forever? Maybe not. But, right now, we're literally in the looney bin, so yeah, if we don't acknowledge that in a way that feels true to us, we won't get better.

So, Kaley and I are going all in on the crazy talk. It makes us laugh. We'll be respectful around other people, but I can't tell you how good it feels to talk about what's going on with someone who gets it, without having to filter ourselves.

I also kind of feel like Zane's Nana would approve, and that makes it even more fun for me. I mean, it's exhausting having to deal with the thoughts in your head that are so intense they cause flashbacks and panic attacks and then, on top of it, having to censor how you talk about it around others. How the heck do they expect you to ever heal?

Kaley grabs my arm, and we lock elbows and walk to the dining room together.

"Dinner was kind of gross tonight," I say to Kaley as we walk toward my room.

"Don't be so loud!" she whispers back with a sneaky giggle as we round the corner and I notice my door is open.

"Hey, I closed that, right?" I ask her as we get closer.

"Yeah, I remember you closing it because we had to turn sideways in order to keep our elbows locked and still get out of the room, and so I specifically remember you pulling the door shut," she replies. Just then, I notice that my blanket is gone.

"Someone was in my room, and they stole my blanket!" I turn to her with total fear in my eyes because

I can feel a major panic attack coming on. Kaley tries to calm me down, but I feel so scared and violated. Someone was in my room, and they took the one thing that made me feel safe. *It's not there. Where could it be? Why would someone take it?* I then see that an elderly patient has it. An orderly is trying to get it from her, and she's holding onto it tight. Like, white-knuckle tight. *Please, please, please don't rip it. It's all I have. It's the thing that makes me feel safe. Oh, god, what's happening? Why does she have it? How did she get it? Please get it back!* I can't fight the panic any longer, and I begin hyperventilating.

Kaley calls a nurse over, and the nurse bends down and says, "You're behaving like a child. It's not that big of a deal. It's just a blanket. Grow up and stop freaking out."

I know, I think in my head as panic won't let words come out of my mouth. *Don't you think I would act rationally if I could? God I hate PTSD! It makes me feel like an idiot.* I can't help it. My throat hurts so bad as I continue to hyperventilate. Kaley moves in between me and the nurse, knowing she's only making things worse. Another nurse comes in with an ice pack and places it on my neck. I don't understand what's happening, but I'm too much in my panic to have any logical thoughts. "You're going to be okay. Just breathe. It's going to be okay. You're safe. Hold the ice on your neck. It's going to be okay." Her voice is so calming, and I begin to feel like I can take actual breaths again.

Panic attacks suck. Not only are they uncontrollable at this point, the initial feeling of not being able to breathe just builds, layer after layer, until I'm hyperventilating so badly that there is no way to slow my breathing. It's like the fear of not being able to breathe makes it harder to breathe, so it's completely counterintuitive. For months now, the only way the really bad attacks would stop would be for me to pass out. But, right now, something is happening with this ice pack on my neck. It's like that compounding effect isn't happening, and I am able to take small breaths. Why has it taken four months for someone to show me this trick? The ice on my neck is helping so much. It's like a magic spell that I can't even describe. These small breaths grow into bigger, deeper breaths, and Kaley runs up to me with my blanket, wraps it around my shoulders, and I begin to calm down.

"I must look like a crazy hot mess," I say as Kaley laughs. The nurse then joins in on the silliness of the situation by laughing as well. "I mean, I may be crazy, but that doesn't mean I don't recognize how silly this all is. I just can't control the flashbacks and panic attacks. But I've been told I might be able to one day, and I'm holding onto that because these things suck," I say with an embarrassed laugh. "What's with the ice?" I ask the nurse.

"Oh, I'm typically a surgical nurse, and we have patients who panic before going into surgery all the time. This is a trick we use on a regular basis. Do you have regular panic attacks?" she asks.

"Daily."

"Wait, and you've never been shown this trick?" she responds.

"No. This is brand-new information. Are you telling me that this trick works every time?"

"Pretty much," she responds and begins to explain that we have the fight-or-flight response built into us for survival, but since we're now civilized, we're typically not going to run away or punch someone when we're in situations that trigger that response. So, the body releases adrenaline in response to our fight-or-flight, but since we aren't running or fighting, it just sits there, causing the chemicals in our body to go a little haywire and resulting in panic attacks. The ice stops the adrenaline from being produced.

"Now for the gross part," she continues, handing me a root beer. "You need to burp the chemical right out of your body."

What?! I think to myself. That is gross and also ridiculous-sounding. But I do it anyway, and you know what? It no longer feels like an elephant is standing on my chest. I feel 100 percent better, other than the fact that I'm exhausted from not being able to breathe, and my throat hurts from gasping for air. Oh, and I feel silly too.

"What the?" I push my way up from the floor. "Why doesn't everyone who deals with mental illness know this trick? I've had at least ten panic attacks since I got here, and you're the first person to share this with me."

"I think most people who deal with mental illness don't think about the physical part of what they're treating. I'm sorry you've been suffering. I'll share this with the other nurses so that if it happens again, they have this tool to deal with it." She smiles as she leaves me and Kaley in my new room.

"I can't thank you enough," I yell after her.

Kaley stays with me a little while longer just to make sure I'm okay, which I am. When she leaves, I pick up my journal to write down this new trick I've learned. This definitely needs to go into my toolbox. I also journal through being misunderstood. I'm so tired of everyone thinking I have control over this stuff. Like it's a conscious decision to be angry with a clearly mentally ill elderly person. I would never do that if I had a choice. God, what kind of monster do they think I am?

As I write and write and write, I take note of the fact that I am clearly getting better because I've been writing for nearly an hour, and I've only gotten stuck twice. That is huge progress. Though the things I'm writing aren't very kind. I decide I will talk to Dr. Anthony tomorrow about how to forgive myself for being sick. I close my journal, run my finger over the embossing, ritualistically, turn my light off, and close my eyes.

Chapter Thirty-Two

"How are you feeling?" Dr. Anthony asks me.

How am I actually doing? I try to come up with an answer, but this couch of Dr. Anthony's is so distractingly uncomfortable that I am having a hard time focusing. The fact that Dr Anthony is sitting in his little wooden chair, leaning forward in anticipation with his piercing blue eyes staring at me waiting for a response, is also not helping. But, even though I'm distracted, I'm still leaps and bounds from where I was when I first got here. Because of regular sleep, I can actually distinguish between my emotions. I can tell if they're coming from my illness or if the situation is causing them. I can identify them with different words, and the coolest part is I have so many tools that I can use to deal with them in healthy ways.

"To say I'm feeling better would be an understatement," I answer back, "I feel like a totally different person. And I'm not just saying that in order to get out of here. I really mean it."

Dr. Anthony smiles and leans back in his chair. "I'm glad to hear that. Now, let's go through your plan for when life gets to be a little too much in the real world. Because, remember, it most likely will. We can't control other people, what they do, or how they treat you. But what's the one thing to remember in situations where others may say something ignorant?"

"That's on them, not me," I answer as if I've rehearsed the line a million times.

"That's right! We can't take their position on our lives personally. Even if they're the most well-intentioned. Mental illness is not something everyone knows enough about to be able to fully understand what you're going through. And, frankly, it's not up to them to bend to your needs, automatically. If you do need something from them, though, you now know how to ask for help. Right?"

"Right."

"Good. It's probably the most important skill you can learn. But, remember, it's important you ask the right person. If you're really struggling with your actual illness, don't depend on your friends to be that help. They may want to, but they are not qualified, and that can put an extra burden on them as well as being dangerous for you. So, if it's just life stuff, lean on your friends. If it's medical, including mental health, lean on your team of professionals. Do you have everyone's contact info?"

"Yeah, I've got it all written down in my journal." I hold the book up and pat the cover.

"Great. Now, let's go over your plan." Dr. Anthony leans over the table in between us, pointing at a printout he made for me. He knows I love a good bullet-point list, and, thankfully, so does he.

I lean in, and we go line by line through what tools to use when and my schedule for outpatient therapy. I have to go twice a week. He also has me seeing a nutritionist because we noticed when I eat certain foods, my moods are drastically different. I have a walking buddy because making sure I get some gentle exercise really helps with the anxiety. All of this in addition to the ice trick, my journal and… singing. I can't wait to get back to singing. Through all of this therapy, we discovered I probably wouldn't have made it as far as I did before coming in here if I wasn't singing. It's a great physical release as well as an emotional release.

"Okay, Nif. I think you're ready. Now remember that most important thing. I know you've been really scared that you'll have to deal with the flashbacks and panic attacks for the rest of your life. But, in the same way you overcame your stutter and inability to read and write, you can heal and overcome the panic attacks and flashbacks. It just might take a bit more time than you'd like." He looks at me with that knowing look. The one that says, "I know you don't like that time piece, but that's just reality, so get over that part." At the same time, I'm looking at him with the look that says, "I don't like that it's going to take time, but I know it's true and am willing to get over that part so I can put in the work to get better."

We both smile, recognizing how far we've come since our first meeting.

"Okay, I feel good about that plan." I pause to take the moment in. It hasn't been easy, and I know I've come a long way. I look Dr. Anthony in the eye and say, "Thank you." Two simple words with more meaning than I can convey, but I can see that Dr. Anthony fully understands.

I walk out of his office and into my room. The room I asked for nearly a week ago. The room where I finally started to take my healing journey seriously. The room that set me on the course to healing. I walk to the window and see that the sun is shining and the snow is melting off the trees. I've taken the cutout magazine pictures of inspiring people and quotes down off the wall and put them in the art therapy room in case someone else can use them. But I've decided to keep the collage I made to remind me of how far I've come.

I sit on the bed next to my folded-up blanket, open up my journal, and begin to write:

Dear Nif,

I want you to remember this moment. The moment when you take your first steps back to the life you've always dreamed of. Remember:

- *all the struggles*
- *not believing you were actually worthy of help*
- *feeling like your situation didn't warrant this diagnosis*
- *not taking care of yourself*
- *not knowing how to ask for help*
- *all the frustration and confusion you felt before this moment.*

Then remember all you've learned. You've got a toolbox full of tips and tricks to use when PTSD strikes and the world gets overwhelming. You've got people like Kaley who truly understand what you're going through and friends and family who will never understand but love you and do the best they can.

Remember that you are strong and capable. Most importantly, remember to ask for help when you need it because you are worthy of being here and life is worth living.

Love, yourself

I'm just finishing when Kaley pops her head in. She sees what I'm doing and lets me finish before saying, "Your parents are here. Are you ready?"

I look up and smile at her. This woman who helped change my life by just being herself. I wonder if she has any idea how incredible she is or how many lives she changes with her attitude toward mental illness. "Well, time to go be crazy on the outside." We both laugh. It's so nice to have someone who absolutely gets what it's like. We hug and start to walk out together.

I see my parents and hug them.

"You ready, kiddo?" my dad asks me as my mom strokes my hair.

"I am." I feel truly confident, and I can tell by the looks on their faces that they can tell.

At the doorway with the sign that says, "No eloping," I pause, turn around, and take it all in. Remembering what I was like just a few short weeks ago and what I'm like now, it's like they're two different people. I smile and turn toward my parents. Each of them puts an arm around me as we walk out the door and head home.

Chapter Thirty-Three

UPBEAT MUSIC COAXES ME AWAKE, JUST ANOTHER TOOL from my toolbox. Since a big part of PTSD is nervous-system-related, I learned that loud noises are very jarring to my system, and if I use fun music to wake up, I start my day off in a much better headspace. I look at the clock. 6 a.m. It's early but I'm determined to stick to the routine I developed in the hospital, and if I'm going to do that, I need the time before school. So, 6 a.m. it is. I literally roll out of bed and onto the floor for a fifteen-minute stretching routine. Once I'm done with that, I get ready for the day. Since anxiety comes from feeling out of control, I do the same things in the same order every day. The list is taped to the wall of my bathroom, and I just go through it, one by one:

- *Stretch*
- *Shower*
- *Brush teeth*
- *Get dressed*
- *Pack lunch*
- *Pack school bag*

I do this while I listen to positive and high-energy music. I then head to the kitchen to have a breakfast that feeds my body with the nutrients it needs to handle any stressors. I know that to my family, this all seems a bit, well, crazy. I wish I could go back to the days when I could just roll out of bed 10 minutes before I would have to leave and grab a Pop-Tart on my way out the door. But I just can't anymore, and one of the things they taught me in the hospital is that if I dwell on how things were before, I can't move forward and heal now.

So, I don't dwell, and I asked my family not to comment on it since it's really hard to stick with this routine anyway. If they make comments, it will be even harder for me. They agreed. The cool thing is that one of the tools in my toolbox is to set my intention for the day. So, where my family and I would have talked about what we were eating or how busy we are, we have decided to start sharing our intentions during breakfast time.

"I know this seems strange to you since this is the first time we're doing this. First, I want to say thank you. It means a lot to me. This daily practice has really helped me the last few weeks in the hospital, so I'm hoping you'll like it too. So, let me explain how to do it. We go around the table, and everyone starts with, 'Today my intention is to…' And then you tell us what your intention is. You can have more than one but definitely need to have one. It can be as simple as intending to have a good or productive day, intending to eat all the vegetables that you packed for lunch, or intending to get up every hour and move your body for five minutes. I'll go first. Today, my intention is to remember that no one at school knows what I'm going through, so I don't expect them to treat me kindly. I will treat myself with kindness so that I don't need others to do it for me."

My family just looks stunned and I kind of smile. I felt the same way when I first heard others who had done this exercise before. It can get real deep and profound. It's such a powerful thing to start the day with intention.

My mom goes next. "My intention is to not run around like a chicken with my head cut off."

Then my dad goes, "My intention is to take three deep breaths each time I'm about to hit record during my recording session today."

Jane giggles and gives Dad two thumbs up because she knows what a big deal that is. My dad tends to hold his breath when recording because he gets so nervous for the performers. It really is something for him to recognize and set an intention to counteract it. Jane goes next. "My intention is not to let Billy get to me today. He's been picking on me, and I want to not care."

We all nod in acknowledgment. "Okay, these are great intentions. We'll check in at dinner tonight and see how we all did. Don't worry if you aren't perfect at it, though," I explain as if I'm a total expert on the subject.

I drop Jane off at school and head to the park. I would normally have a study hall first period, but today, I am scheduled to meet my new walking buddy to talk about our goals, our schedules, and to just meet in general. Dr. Anthony set it up. I've never heard of a walking buddy, but I've learned to trust him and am willing to try anything.

It's a gorgeous winter day. The snow can be seen for miles, but the sun is shining, and it feels really good on my face. After weeks of being locked in a building, I am enjoying being outside in a way I never thought I would. Other than the elderly couple sitting on the bench across from the gazebo, I'm the only one there. I climb on top of the picnic table and pull out my journal to write just as a woman approaches. "Nif?"

"Oh, hi. Yes, that's me. I'm Nif." I stretch out my hand to shake hers. She does the same.

"Hi, I'm Hannah. It's nice to meet you."

I smile at her. She's so nice. She has long dark hair that she's pulled up into a messy bun on top of her head. She's got just this totally chill, hippie vibe that I love. I immediately feel at ease.

"Do you live in the area?" I ask because the town is so small that I feel like I would have seen her before.

"I do. I live just outside of town. But I work in Kenton, so I do almost everything there. I'm assuming you asked because you haven't seen me around." She looks at me with a knowing smirk on her face.

"That's exactly why I asked," I respond with a chuckle.

"So, Dr. Anthony tells me that you and I have a lot in common," she begins.

"Oh, really? He didn't say anything to me. He just said it's a good idea to have a walking buddy to keep me accountable and that he knew someone, you."

"Oh, he's tricky like that."

"What do we have in common?" I ask.

"He isn't allowed to come out and tell me because of privacy laws, so I'm not 100 percent sure. But, having worked with him for as long as I have, I have a pretty good idea. Why don't we start with you sharing whatever you're comfortable sharing and go from there? Sound good?"

"Sure, I have post-traumatic stress disorder."

"So did I."

"*Did?*" I respond, so intrigued. What does she mean, *did?*

"Yep, did," she responds. "Am I to assume that you were told this was a lifelong diagnosis?" I nod, and she continues, "Yeah, me too. It's just not true. I was diagnosed ten years ago. And I haven't had a flashback in about five years. It took a lot of therapy and work, but it makes me so frustrated that they say you'll have something that's treatable forever."

I am glued to every word that comes out of this woman's mouth. She is literally the epitome of hope for me, and I can't believe it. I feel so much relief just listening as she continues.

"Look, you're definitely going to be more sensitive to things in the future, but the idea of a life sentence of panic attacks, flashbacks, and nightmares just isn't true. I look at it this way. If you break your leg, that's what the initial cause of your PTSD is. Then, you get your leg set. For you, that was going into the hospital where you got a lot of tools to help you deal with it—so, kind of like a cast, right?" I nod. "Then you get the cast off and have to go to physical therapy—your weekly therapy. I'm assuming you'll have to go to weekly therapy, right?" I nod again. "Then your leg gets stronger, but you might be a bit more prone to injury in the future. Right? Like those guys who are always saying, 'Oh, it's an old football injury.' Right? Does that make sense?"

"It makes total sense," I say to her with awe in my voice. I've never had anyone explain it that way to me before, and I have more hope that I can get through this than I've ever had. I can't wait for this woman to be my walking buddy. Not only is she going to keep me moving physically, she seems to be someone who can help if I get stuck with my PTSD.

She seems to see that I'm in awe of her and abruptly says as she claps her hands together loudly, "Okay! Let's get to walking."

I jerk back to the current situation, smile, and hop off the picnic table. "Okay." And we start off down the path.

Chapter Thirty-Four

I HEAR THE BELL RING FROM MY CAR. I'M WAITING FOR everyone to get settled before I go in. My goal is to talk to Mrs. M during second period and then start my actual school day during third period. I don't want to be distracted, and I have to check in with the office, so the timing has to be perfect. That was the first bell, and I can see everyone hustling to their next class. I am longing for the days when a pop quiz or whether I would get an A on my history test were my biggest concerns.

Those days are now replaced with paying attention to what I eat and how much I sleep so that my body doesn't accidentally go into fight-or-flight mode. Which leads me to being unable to control what my body does and ending up back in the hospital. I give my head a little shake. *No, Nif! Don't go there. It's not worth dwelling on. That's just not your reality anymore. But remember what Dr. Anthony said—with some discipline and diligence, you can get better. That's what you need to focus on.* I take a deep breath as the second bell rings. I gather my things and my determination and head inside.

UGH! Getting through the office process of reenrolling and all the paperwork is like nothing I can explain nor do I want to, if I'm being honest. Sometimes being out of the hospital makes me want to go back in. But I get through it and leave as politely as I can. I'll remind you the office workers are super gossips, so trying to keep anything private takes the will of a thousand Olympic athletes.

GOD, WHY ARE YOU SO NERVOUS? I yell at myself as I try to shake the nerves out of my body. *Mrs. M will understand. I mean, you have a pretty serious condition. Yeah, but you let her down more than once, and she's got a whole choir to think about. Well, all you can do is ask and state your case. You've got way more tools to deal with your condition now than you did before. You can handle this, and you won't let her down. You just have to tell her that. You can do it!* I hesitantly reach for the choir room door but stop when I hear Mrs. M talking to someone. I'd recognize that voice anywhere. Jessa. It sounds like they're finishing up, so I wait outside the door, knowing that she'd have her ear pressed up against it if it was her instead of me. But, after the year I've had, I opt to give her privacy. Whatever she has going on is none of my business. I put my back against the wall and slowly slide to the ground. I pull out my journal, run my fingers across the top as I do every time I'm about to write in it, and open the book. I'm about to start writing when the choir room doors flings open, and Jessa comes out in a huff. She sees me and gives me a glare that would freeze someone who's just come out of a sauna, immediately. She continues toward the bathroom, and I get up, grab my bag, and walk to the door.

It's still open, but I knock on the doorframe meekly. "Hi, Mrs. M. Got a minute?"

Come on, Nif! If you're not confident, why would she be confident in you? Buck up. This is your future we're talking about here. Show her you're better and you can do this!

Mrs. M gestures for me to come in. "Nif! I'm so happy to see you back. You look great. What a relief. I was really worried about you."

I clear my throat and, with much more confidence, say, "Hi, Mrs. M. Thank you. Yes, I'm feeling *much* better." I emphasize *much* in the hopes that she understands that I am all better, no doubt about it. I'm back at full strength. Even though I'm having trouble convincing myself of that at the moment. But I am determined to exude confidence so, I continue.

"Mrs. M, I am better. I mean, I still have to go to therapy and check in with the doctor from the hospital every week, but that's just a formality."

WHY ARE YOU SAYING THIS?! SHUT UP! SHE DOESN'T NEED TO KNOW. Oh god, now she's never going to trust you. You literally just admitted to being a crazy person.

I gather myself and try again. "I wanted to talk to you about the spring concert."

Mrs. M gives me a knowing look like she was expecting this. "Of course, dear, I was hoping you'd stop by. I've been thinking about this a lot."

"You have?" I ask, pondering the idea that Mrs. M would think of me at all when I wasn't right in front of her.

"Of course. I thought of you often while you were away. It's just so good to see you doing better. But are you sure you're *better* better?" she asks.

There it is. She doesn't trust me. I can feel the blood leave my face. I feel like I might cry. Not being in the spring concert would be a fate worse than anything I just went through. I mean, I'm a senior. It's my last high school concert, ever! I worked really hard to get better; I deserve a shot at this. Ugh.

Mrs. M can see that I'm having a thought spiral. She's very used to them. I wish I could blame them on

PTSD, but the truth is I've always been like this. I just get completely stuck in my head sometimes.

"Of course, I know it's your last high school concert, and you've been working so hard to get better," Mrs. M chimes in to try and break the spiral.

But, instead of breaking it, my brain immediately goes to, *Is she a psychic? How does she know my exact thoughts? Okay, Nif, calm down. She doesn't know those are your exact thoughts. Those are just the most logical thoughts anyone could have about this situation. SNAP OUT OF IT!*

"Yes, that's exactly what I was going to say. I have been working so hard, and the doctor I was seeing in the hospital thinks I'm doing much better. He's given me a walking buddy so I can deal with any stress that might come up while I work to heal the trauma, and I'm hopeful. I would just die if I couldn't sing in the spring concert this year. Do you think there's a place for me?"

I think it's going to be an easy and quick conversation, but my hopes of that happening are shattered when Mrs. M walks over to the choir chairs that are lined up in semicircle rows all around the room, sits down, and gestures to me to do the same.

I do, and we end up talking for fifteen more minutes. Mrs. M expresses her concerns, asks me about my treatment and progress, and just feelings about the way things are going in general. It feels really nice to have a conversation with her. She is one of those special people who can make you feel at ease and has no malicious judgment about her.

Once I get through telling her about my treatment and my plan moving forward, Mrs. M stands up abruptly, straightens her skirt, and says, "Well then, let's have a listen, shall we?" She walks toward the piano and hands me some sheet music.

I'm flabbergasted as I look it over. "Does this mean I can have a solo?"

She smiles slightly and then gets all proper and replies, "If you can still sing, we'll consider it."

I take a moment to look over the music while Mrs. M punches the notes out on the piano. It's been a while since I've done a cold audition, but I want to have a solo in the spring concert so bad that it hurts. So, I focus as hard as I can and nod at Mrs. M that I'm good to go, she punches out the intro on the piano, and I break out into song.

The piece is full of soul and passion, it's right in my range's sweet spot, and I am in heaven as I belt out each and every note with the confidence one might have if they've sung a piece a thousand times. It's like something outside of me is guiding my performance, and when it's over, both Mrs. M and I break out in gleeful laughter knowing that solo is absolutely mine.

Mrs. M gets up from behind the piano with a serious look on her face, grabs my hands in hers, and says, "Nif, this solo was made for you, and you can have it under one condition."

I look her straight in the eyes waiting to hear what it is, hoping it's something I can actually do, and she continues. "I absolutely need your word that you will be open and honest with me about what's going on with you. If you get too stressed, you have to tell me. I promise you being stressed won't mean you automatically have to give up the solo. If you get overwhelmed, we will figure out a way to help you so that you can give your best performance ever in front of everyone at the spring concert. Do you promise?"

Who is this woman, and how am I lucky enough to be her student? She really is one of the good ones. "I promise," I give her hand a little squeeze, "and thank you for being willing to not only give me another chance, but to work with me if my condition gets the best of me. You won't regret it."

Chapter Thirty-Five

THE MOMENT IS BROKEN WHEN THE DOORS TO THE choir room fly open, and Jessa comes barreling in with the energy of a team of Clydesdales.

She looks super angry when she yells, "That solo was supposed to be mine!" She goes straight up to Mrs. M, gets right in her face, and continues yelling, "This isn't fair! She hasn't even been here for weeks! She doesn't deserve it, and you know I'm the better singer. Just wait until my mother hears about this!"

The whole time she's yelling, I can feel my anxiety start to creep up, but I take a deep breath—thank goodness no one notices—and muster up the courage to interrupt, "Hey! Leave her alone. Who do you think you are talking to like that? The choir is *hers* to run, not yours."

I have never seen someone turn such a deep shade of red as I am seeing right now as Jessa puts her arms straight down by her side, leans forward, and yells, "I WISH YOU WOULD HAVE DIED! You're a nobody who just keeps getting in my way, and I'm sick of it. You no-talent, entitled, little piece of…"

Mrs. M cuts her off with a very loud and very stern, "That's enough, Jessa."

"No, you know what, Mrs. M, thank you, but I've got this." I turn away from her toward Jessa. I look her straight in the eye and, with the same amount of energy, I say, "You know what, Jessa, I'm not the entitled one. I don't know what your problem is, but *my* problem with you is that you think you're better than everyone else. You think you should just get the solo because you happen to be able to hit the notes. Guess what? Being able to sing is not the same as being good at singing. And even if it was, you're not the only one who can sing. Also, maybe it's time you stop focusing so much on what everyone else is doing or how they're getting things you aren't, and start focusing on what you're doing to better your life. Because let me tell you, the world is much bigger than this puny little town, and you won't always have your mummy to run and cry to. Essentially, Jessa, GROW UP!

"Thank you, Mrs. M. I'll talk to you later." I flip my hair, turn on my heel in true Jessa fashion, and walk out. With my head held the highest it's ever been, I walk into the hallway and clutch my journal, knowing it's only because of the work I've done that I was able to finally stand up for myself. My heart is racing when I see Zane and Karsten in front of an entire group of students, all looking shocked because they could hear Jessa and me in the hallway. Zane and Karsten walk up to me and ask if I'm okay. "I'm fine. That was a long time coming. Don't you think?"

Just then, someone starts to clap. It's just one and slow at first, but then another joins and another, and all of a sudden, the whole group is clapping and hollering and cheering. I had no idea how many kids Jessa tortured. I thought it was just me, but standing there with this group of other kids, feeling a collective sense of relief, I knew I wasn't alone. I began to smile and relax. *I will never let her get to me again.*

The group breaks up, and Zane and Karsten are left standing there looking at me. I realize just how special our friendship is and how much I love them.

"Listen, guys, I owe you both a huge apology. I have not been good to you since the crash. I've pushed you away, tried to control you, was downright mean to you, and you were only trying to help. It's no excuse, but apparently, it's all part of my condition. And now that I know, I will work really hard to identify when those behaviors are happening and use the insane, pun intended, toolbox I have now to stop myself." We all giggle a little, and then Karsten and Zane stop and look at each other.

"Is it okay to laugh at this?" Zane asks, truly concerned.

"Hey, if you can't laugh in times like this, it'll make you crazy," I say back.

We giggle some more.

"But, seriously, you two, I really am so sorry. You're better friends than anyone could hope for and definitely more than I could ever imagine. So, I'm going to do better." I finish my apology.

Zane chimes in. "I'd be so interested in all these, what would you call them, symptoms? If we know them, maybe we can help point them out and just make sure it really isn't something we're doing. We're not perfect either, you know, and friendship is a two, or, in our case, three-way street."

Karsten excitedly adds, "Yeah! What a great idea, Zane. And I wonder if this would be something other kids might like to know about? Maybe you could do some sort of assembly."

"You just want to get out of class," Zane teases.

"I mean, that would be an added benefit, for sure." Karsten gestures as if this was a thought he'd never had, but we all know this thought is always on his mind.

We all laugh, but I think Karsten might be onto something.

Chapter Thirty-Six

I AM STARING AT THE GIANT CLOCK MOUNTED ON THE ceiling of the front office, growing more and more nervous with each click of the second hand. I jump when Mrs. Clark says, "Principal Morgan will see you now." I pull my journal to my chest, not only for courage, but because my notes are in it. Zane, Karsten, and I have been putting together this pitch for the principal for over a week. Ever since the day I stood up to Jessa.

We walk in with pep in our steps and hope that we might be able to do something good.

Principal Morgan sits behind her mahogany desk in a large leather chair. Her office looks like it should be at Oxford college in England, not Small Town, USA, Karlville. I am intimidated but also feel like she's trying too hard. I can't believe this small, in more ways than one, woman stands between me and my ability to help so many kids. I am so sick of this feeling. I can't wait to graduate and get to decide what I do on my own.

But my parents both reminded me last night that even they don't get to do everything they want to do. And that I shouldn't have a "defeatist attitude," which basically means that I need to look on the bright side and assume things will work out. Holding my journal and running my fingers over the embossed letters, I begin the presentation.

"Did you know that according to the DCO, a study done just last year showed that, approximately four in ten teens have a mental disorder and approximately one in five seriously considered attempting suicide? Those may not seem like large numbers, but when you consider the effects it has on their family and friends, I think it's safe to say that everyone is affected."

Principal Morgan responds with, "Okay, what does that have to do with me?"

I reply, "Well, since I've gone through, well, all that I've gone through this year, we—" I make a sweeping gesture to include myself, Karsten and Zane, "think it would be helpful if I were to give a speech at the beginning of our spring concert assembly next month."

Just looking at her face, you can see she is fuming. She is not the type of person who ever wants to talk about what's actually going on with us. We students talk about it all the time. At this point, I realize she has been quiet for a while, and I haven't breathed. So, I let out a breath, and it seems to break the tension.

Zane chimes in with, "Yeah, Mrs. Morgan, we think it could really help. Nif was able to explain her condition and some of the symptoms to us the other day, and it helped so much. We didn't even realize it was…"

Mrs. Morgan interrupts her. "Well, I can't possibly give you permission to do this. The assembly is supposed to be a celebration, and this would just bring it down."

"Mrs. Morgan," Karsten says in a very authoritative voice, "we, your students, are asking you to allow us to do something that is very important to us. Something that could help and we won't take no for an answer."

I just sit down in a chair and beam with pride, at this point. Karsten has been talking about using his "senior" voice all year, and I think Zane and I are experiencing it for ourselves for the first time. It's kind of awesome. His whole take has been, what are they going to do? Kick me out of school?

Mrs. Morgan seems to understand that she isn't going to get rid of us or this conversation easily, so she pulls the only card she has left and in the most cowardly way says, "Well, I can't possibly approve this without the school board signing off on it." She seems proud of herself and is not expecting our response.

All three of us get up and plant our feet so we're looking squarely at her face. We anticipated this, and I say, "Great. The next meeting is tomorrow night, right? I'll be sure we're added to the agenda." All three of us turn as if it's a rehearsed dance move and walk out.

When we're clear of any prying eyes or ears, we high five each other, hug, and congratulate ourselves. We did it!

"Okay, team, next step is to rally the troops," I say in my best rally voice as we head off to our media class to do the TV show.

Chapter Thirty-Seven

THE ROOM IS ABUZZ WITH ENERGY AND EXCITEMENT as it always is when we're about to go live. But the butterflies in my stomach are bigger than they've ever been. I haven't gone live since the broadcast where Zane had to help me out because I couldn't read.

Just remember all that you've been through. I mean, really think about it. You lost your actual mind, and now you're back and better than ever! You just need to show the school that. And if anyone picks on you for any of this, remember that 'hurt people hurt other people, and it's not about you—it's about them.' I know, I know, the clichés we have to tell ourselves sometimes. But clichés work for me so I will absolutely continue to tell them to myself.

I'm sitting in the makeup chair with Karsten frantically primping around me with more energy than usual. "I'm so excited to be able to do your hair and makeup again, giiiirrrll. This has been a long time coming." He gives me a little hug as Zane hands me the script, and I am so relieved when I can read every word, and I see the look of relief on her face when she recognizes that I can too.

"Places, everyone," I hear from the other area of the room. I give myself a quick little "you can do this" look in the mirror and turn to walk toward the set when Zane and Karsten come running up with their arms stretched out.

"Group hug!" Karsten yells, and we do our group hug thing. It feels amazing.

"Stop, you're going to make me cry."

"Do not ruin that makeup," Karsten says with a stern but joking look on his face.

I get to my seat and look at the entire crew. They're all mouthing some form of encouragement like, "You can do this. You got this." I am the luckiest person in the world. I look over at my coanchor as he begins to read the script on the teleprompter. Eventually, he hands it over to me, and I begin. "As most of you know, I've struggled with post-traumatic stress disorder this year due to the farmers' market crash. It hasn't been an easy road, but thanks to so much support, I'm on the track of healing. I've learned so much about mental health through this journey, and I've learned that statistically, a lot of you are dealing with things that you aren't sharing. Because of this, I've asked Principal Morgan if I can speak at the assembly before the spring concert and give you all some tools I've learned this year. She doesn't seem to think this is important and has pushed it off on the school board. She has said the only way that can happen is if we get school board permission. Well, their next meeting is tomorrow night. I know it's last minute, but I'm hoping this topic is as important to you as it is to me and that you'll cancel whatever plans you have and join me as I ask the school board to put our mental health on the agenda. The details are on our school's website. Please, everyone, this might save someone's life."

I can see that the entire crew is just staring at me. There's nothing left for me to read, but the camera is still on my face. I just think to myself, *Don't break contact with the camera. They need to understand how important this is. 20 percent of teens think about suicide. Keep going.* The director finally realizes the camera is still on. You can hear a pin drop when he motions to the cameraperson to cut.

The entire room erupts in applause, and everyone is talking about how they're going to cancel their plans and be there. "Should we make signs?" I hear one person ask the people around her. I just smile. I'm so relieved everyone feels as strongly about this as I do. Sometimes when you're going through something so seemingly uncommon, you think you're all alone. At this moment, I realize I'm not, and it feels really good. Then I realize it's also really sad and vow to make as big a difference as I can in the world because of this experience.

Chapter Thirty-Eight

I PUT MY CAR IN PARK, TAKE A DEEP BREATH, OPEN THE door, and head towards the entry to the high school. I've never been to a school board meeting and am definitely feeling nervous. *It's going to be fine. Mom and Dad will meet you inside; so will Karsten and Zane. You won't be alone. They're only human. They put their pants on one leg at a time, just like everyone else. And, besides, you're trying to do a good thing. How could they say no to that?* I tell myself as I go to open the big double doors at the front of the building.

The door creaks open, and what I see when I get inside is unlike anything I could have ever expected. There's a huge group of angry parents and their kids standing with signs in a mob outside the room where the board meeting is about to start.

"There she is!" someone yells, and the mob comes toward me, screaming that I'm crazy and psycho and shouldn't be allowed in school, let alone allowed to talk to the entire student body about mental health.

My body tenses up. I can feel the panic start to swell inside. I am so overwhelmed that I can't even do the breathing exercises I've been taught to do when I feel a flashback coming on. Just then, I feel someone throw something over my head, grab my shoulders, and guide me to the bathroom. They immediately take the object off my head, and I see my parents, Zane, and Karsten standing in front of me. Karsten goes to block the door, while Zane and my parents try to calm me down.

"Oh, Nif," my mom says, trying to comfort me, "we had no idea this was going to happen, sweetie."

"What is this?" I ask, completely confused but starting to regain my regular breathing.

"Flipping Jessa watched the school news broadcast and decided to tell her mom that you were trying to encourage the other students to *pretend* to be crazy. Since, you know, clearly, you're only doing all of this PTSD stuff for attention," Zane explains in her most exasperated, *I hate that girl, why is she such a pain* voice.

"Are you serious?" I plead. "Does she really think this is how I want attention? I mean, you know, seeing people die every time I close my eyes and not being able to stop crying, let alone stop my body from essentially convulsing, is not my idea of a great way to get attention. She's so stupid if she thinks that."

"Yeah, well, she is stupid, and she does think that, and now her mom has gotten all the other parents with kids who are just as obnoxious as her on board to protest your talking to the school board," Karsten yells from the door where he's literally having to hold off an angry mob from storming in. It's like a scene out of a witch hunt movie.

I try to process all of it. It's just so unreal. I take a few minutes to just be quiet and then… "You know what? It's people like this that stop people with real mental health issues from speaking up and getting the help they need. If I don't do something, I could literally be helping them kill someone. Because there are a lot of people, kids, who think suicide is the only way out. Well, not today, y'all. These people are just going to have to let me speak. And, if the school board decides I am not able to talk to the school at the spring assembly, then I'll just have to find another way to get the message out. I can't tell you how scared I've been through all of this, but at least I had you guys. Some kids don't have anyone. Nope. I won't be silenced."

I gather myself, look in the mirror, and say, "You got this." I walk past Zane and my parents. "I'm going to be fine. Don't worry." They look at me with pride, and it gives me strength. "Okay, Karsten, let go." He does, and I open the door, and a few of the protestors banging fall into the bathroom.

I stand up straight, keep my eyes forward, and say absolutely nothing as I push my way through with complete determination. Some move, some don't, but I find a way around them anyway until I get to the door of the board meeting room where Jessa and her mom have firmly planted themselves to block me from entering. I look Jessa straight in the eyes with a "get out of my way, you pathetic, sad human" look on my face. She seems to understand that things will definitely get bad for her if she doesn't let me through, so she moves aside. I walk into the room to see friendly faces packed to the rafters. The students from the TV station are there with a camera setup so they can livestream, and they've brought more students than I could have imagined to fill the room with supportive faces. It seems they got there much earlier, and the room was too full for the protestors to get in. Either that or they just blocked them from getting in. They open the doors so Zane, Karsten and my parents can join me inside, and we make our way to the front.

As I walk down the aisle, people are grabbing my hands and saying encouraging words, and I feel so full of love and support that I almost cry. *Knock it off, Nif. You don't want to give the school board any reason to doubt your strength.* I find my place in the front row.

The doors open again with Jessa, being rude as ever, trying to walk through the mob. "Let me in, you weirdo. I'm on the agenda too."

One of the school board members in front of the room commands them to let her in, and they do. Another member bangs the gavel, and the meeting begins.

"It's nice to see such a lively group of students here tonight," one of the members says, starting the meeting with an awkward chuckle.

Since we are a late addition and it seems the school board is taking the opportunity to show its students what a board meeting is like, we are last on the agenda.

We had done a little recon before the meeting, and we knew there were two members that we most likely wouldn't have to convince. One is a medical doctor, and the other is a psychologist. But there are still three that are definitely wildcards, and according to Zane and Karsten, at least two of them are really good friends with Jessa's mom.

After an hour and a half, I hear, "The board will now hear from Jennifer Matthews."

Zane nudges my side, and I stand and walk to the podium. "It's Nif," I say meekly, looking at the floor.

"Excuse me, young lady, what did you say?" The board member with the gavel is looking to me as I shuffle a bit with nervousness.

"GO, NIF!" one of the audience members yells out, and I turn to look at them. Each of their faces stare back at me with the hope that they'll be heard too, and I feel a surge of confidence. I straighten my shoulders and begin…

"Hello, board members, my name is Nif, and I'm here today to talk to you about mental health in teens and to ask permission to give a speech at our spring assembly addressing some of these issues. As I explained to Mrs. Morgan, approximately four in ten teens have a mental disorder, and approximately one in five seriously considers attempting suicide. And, as you can see," I make a sweeping motion to indicate all the people in the room, "this is a very important topic to myself and my fellow students."

Fifteen minutes later, I say, "Yes, if you allow me to give my speech, I will send you a copy as soon as I've written it for approval and promise not to give out any medical advice. Thank you!" I turn to walk back to my seat, feeling relieved and still full of adrenaline. Applause begins to erupt but is immediately shot down by the board,

"The board will now hear Jessa Conway." Jessa walks to the podium, insulting anyone who gets in her way in the crowded room, which is a lot. Her mother follows close behind and finds a spot off to the side of the room, where she stands staring at Jessa with her arms crossed.

Jessa looks nervous as she looks toward her mother and then back to the board. She fumbles, and her notes fall to the ground. I almost feel sorry for her. Her mother clearly intimidates her. It reminds me of something my therapist always says, "Hurt people hurt other people." *Maybe that's why Jessa is always so awful to everyone else. Is it because her mother is so awful to her?*

My thoughts are cut off when I hear one of the board members say, "Young lady, we don't find your concerns valid. Please take a seat." Jessa looks over to her mother, who is clearly angry as her face turns redder and redder. She attempts to talk back to the board and is shut down immediately with, "Nif will be allowed to give her speech." The gavel rings out, and the crowd in the room cheers so loudly my ears are ringing as everyone in the room makes their way over to congratulate me.

My parents come over and give me a giant hug. At the same time, I catch a glimpse of Jessa's mom scolding her on their way out of the room. Jessa just hangs her head in embarrassment. I wonder if I'll ever understand how those two can live their lives just trying to bring others down. It honestly feels like their main purpose, and it makes me kind of sad. But then I think, *You don't have to understand. Soon you'll be living your dream in Los Angeles.* A smile spreads across my face as my parents squeeze even harder.

"We're so proud of you, Nif." My dad's words are muffled as he buries his face in my hair.

The room clears, and it's just me, Karsten, and Zane left standing and staring at the table where the board was sitting.

The three of us look at each other, break out into laughter, grab each other for a group hug, and dance round and round and round.

"I can't believe it worked," Zane exclaims.

"I can't believe we had to fight for it to work," Karsten replies.

"I can't believe I now have to give a speech about the darkest time in my life to the entire school," I chime in. We all pause. "But it's going to help people so… all good," I add.

We dance some more.

Chapter Thirty-Nine

It's been a couple weeks since the board meeting, and I've been working on my speech, which was approved by both the board members in the health industries without issue. I've also been rehearsing for the spring assembly and concert every day. I'm feeling pretty good about it. I'm finding just about as much enjoyment in speaking as I am in singing, which definitely surprises me. My parents have been unbelievably supportive and have even hired a speech coach to help me out. The exercises speech coaches use to help their speakers calm their nervous system down are very similar to some that I've learned in therapy, so it's all kind of coming together to reinforce my healing process.

The solo I get to do for the spring concert is probably my favorite of all time. Every time I sing it full out, it's so passion-filled and right in my sweet spot range-wise that it's almost like my body goes through a good cry and releases all tension I'm holding onto. It's an amazing experience.

Right now, I'm alone in the choir room. It's about an hour before school starts, so it's quiet. Mrs. M opened the doors for me but left a few minutes ago to go run some copies down in the office. I have the whole space to myself. I plug my background track into the surround sound speakers and begin to practice when the grand piano lid suddenly falls, creating a really loud BANG. I immediately drop to the ground in a way that has now become all too familiar. I am having a flashback. I am back at the crash, unable to move or yell for help. All the events of that day play through as if I'm there.

But, because of my therapy, I've now learned not to fight the flashback, and as a result, it hurts less physically and is less intense emotionally. Mrs. M comes rushing through the door and finds me on the ground gasping for air. Because of all the work I've done, one thing I started doing was warning people about my flashbacks and letting them know what to do when I have one in their presence. The simple act of warning them that a flashback might happen has helped me so much.

I think the fear of having a flashback around other people and potentially traumatizing them was creating so much worry that the stress of it mixed with the genuine PTSD was making them happen more and more, and they were much more intense. Once I started telling people what was up, the flashbacks started decreasing in amount and intensity. So, at this moment, Mrs. M knows exactly what to do. She sits quietly, holding my head, keeping her breathing calm, which helps calm me down, and the flashback ends relatively quickly.

As I come back to the present, I look at Mrs. M. "Are you okay?" she asks.

"Yeah. I hate those things, but they're getting better so that's good," I reply.

I make my way to my feet and shut the background track off. "The piano lid slammed shut unexpectedly, and that's what caused it," I explain. Mrs. M nods that she understands. "I'd love to get a little more practice in, if that's okay."

"Sure thing. I'll be in my office if you need anything."

Alone in the room, I look down at my hand. It's shaking. *Can I actually pull this off? I mean, that was just one loud noise. Performing in front of everyone is going to be so much more... well, everything. Oh god, what if I have another flashback on stage? I won't be able to recover from that.*

I decide to just go to class. I shout "goodbye" to Mrs. M. and head out for the day.

Chapter Forty

That night, as I'm cleaning the kitchen after dinner, my mom and dad go to the living room to watch the local news. As part of my therapy, the doctors have advised that I stay away from watching the news, as it's full of things that used to give me nightmares. I don't feel as informed, but I definitely feel better about life.

"Hey, Nif, come in here," my mom yells from the living room right as Jane comes into the kitchen and starts pulling on my shirt. "They're talking about you!"

"What are you talking about?" I come around the corner right as the news flashes a picture of me and then cuts to footage of the board meeting. The footage goes up into the corner of the screen to reveal that Karen Kolby, the reporter I was going to meet the day of the crash, is doing a story about my assembly speech. She's inviting everyone to go see me speak, and I am frozen.

I try to listen to what she's saying, but I can feel the panic rise up in me. I honestly don't know what to do, so I just run to my room and slam my door.

You're going to be OKAY. The crash will not happen again. The fear you're feeling isn't from anything happening right now. It's all just part of your condition. You're going to be OKAY, I whisper, coaxing myself out of it. I pick up my phone and call Zane. "I really need you to come over," I plead, barely holding it together but remembering that, when this happens, I need to ask for help.

"Nif, are you okay?" my mom asks through the door.

"Yeah, I'm okay, Mom. Thanks. Zane is going to come over for a little bit, though, if that's okay," I say back without feeling the guilt I used to feel for needing to talk to my friends instead of her. My parents have been so incredible through this whole experience, and part of what they've done is go to therapy with me so we could create what the doctors call a "crisis plan," which is really just a plan for when I can't handle certain things. Sometimes those things are better addressed with my parents, and sometimes they're better addressed with my friends.

Since we've been able to do this together, there are no hurt feelings, and I don't feel guilty. Zane shows up with Karsten, and we all lock ourselves away in my room.

A few minutes later, I hear my family walk back to the living room.

Zane asks, "What's going on?" as Karsten sits on the bed with his arm around me.

"You guys, I don't think I can do this." They both look at me like, "don't be an idiot."

"What are you talking about?" Karsten asks, trying not to be his sassy self.

"That reporter, the one from the crash, Karen Kolby…" I begin.

"What did that B-word do now?" Karsten interrupts. "Do I need to pound on her a little?" He continues punching his fist into his hand.

"No, no, nothing like that, but she just told everyone on LIVE TV about my meeting with the school board and how they should all come out to support me at my speech! Can you believe it?"

"Sweetie, that's great!" Karsten says enthusiastically.

"*Great?!* You did hear what I said, right? She told *everyone* that I was going to talk about being crazy. EVERYONE! And now, complete strangers might show up at school and—and—and I just don't think I can do this!" I can't help it, and I start to hyperventilate.

"Okay, Okay, calm down. Deep breaths." Zane coaxes me back to the present. "It's going to be okay. I promise."

"Nif, I know this seems scary, but this is so awesome! If the news is inviting people out, they might show up themselves and report on it. Your speech might impact even more people, and isn't that what you said you wanted?" Karsten says.

"I know you're right, but what if I have another flashback? You guys, I don't think I can handle that. I really don't. I just don't think I'm strong enough."

"Okay, well, that's ridiculous," Zane responds super matter-of-factly. "Look at all you've been through, and you're not only still here—you're giving a speech about it in the hopes that you'll help others, and you're going to sing your heart out at the last concert of your high school career."

"No pressure," I reply back sarcastically.

Zane and Karsten look at each other as if they have a huge secret.

"Did you bring it?" Karsten asks Zane.

"I kind of thought we might need it."

"What are you two talking about?"

Karsten sits up straight on the edge of the bed and claps his hands excitedly as Zane pulls out a little mesh pouch from her pocket.

"Well, we've seen you carrying your journal around and," Zane puts her hand to her heart, "it just means the world to me how you've embraced my nana's saying and are using it not only to give yourself strength, but now are going to spread the message to give other people strength too. It really means the world to me. And I told Nana about it, and she is just over the moon too. Anyway, we know that journal is going to fill up, and it's a bit cumbersome, so it's not the most practical way to remind you to have aggressive optimism, so we had this made for you."

She hands me the pouch, and I open it, and a little silver ring falls into the palm of my hand. It's shaped like a heart and has the letters "AO" engraved on it.

"Whaaaaat is this?" I squeal. "I absolutely love it! This is insanely thoughtful. I'm going to wear it every single day of my life. I can't believe you two. Wow. I honestly could not have asked for better friends." We group hug on the bed and get up to dance in a circle. We stop, and I put the ring on my right middle finger, stretch my hand out in front of me, and just stare at it for a minute. "This is absolutely perfect! It's almost like a superhero ring. If anyone sends negativity my way, I can just show them my ring." I gesture by showing the middle finger. We all laugh, and I look at the two of them, feeling so grateful that I called for help. I feel stronger than ever and recommit to doing everything I can to help others who might be going through things they don't know how to handle.

Chapter Forty-One

YOU CAN DO THIS. YOU ARE STRONGER THAN YOU KNOW. You continue to prove to yourself how strong you are. I mean, did you ever think you would get back here? No, no, you didn't. And yet here you are, proving you have a history of underestimating yourself. So, just knock that underestimating crap off right now. Okay. Okay, I will. I peek through the heavy velvet blue curtains to see a packed house. I try not to throw up, but can feel the chunks start to rise in my throat. I turn the aggressive optimism ring over and over on my finger as I feel the cool metal on my skin to remind myself of how strong I am. Still, I find I'm getting stuck in my head.

"Niiiiifffff!" I hear Karsten squeal. I am so grateful to hear his voice because I was seriously close to throwing up everywhere. I turn around to see him and Zane standing there looking like they both swallowed canaries, holding their sweaters tightly closed.

"What are you two up to? Why are you wearing sweaters? It's like a thousand degrees in here," I ask right as they're about to pop because they can't hold it in anymore. They open their sweaters to reveal matching, yellow "Aggressive Optimism" t-shirts.

"Oh my gosh, you guys!" I squeal. "You two are the sweetest humans on the planet. I just can't with you. You two are the best! I can't believe you did this! It's so nice. Will you sit close to the stage in case I need the reminder?"

They both look at each other and get the same "I've got a secret" look on their faces, and they say in unison, "We won't have to!"

"What do you mean?"

"Look!" Zane peels back the curtain, and Karsten gestures to someone in the audience, who then gestures to the entire first five rows. They all stand up in unison, and I notice they're all the same kids who were in the room at the board meeting, the ones who were so supportive. They all take their sweaters off to reveal they're all wearing the same t-shirts as Zane and Karsten.

I blow them air kisses and mouth thank you as big as I can and then have to back away because I don't want them to see me cry. The tears are pouring out of me, and my body erupts in sobs. I am so overwhelmed with love and support, and I just don't know what to do with all the emotion. Even though the tears have become a common occurrence in my life this year, this time feels so different. Warm and safe, instead of dark and scary. Karsten gives an enthusiastic thumbs up, and Zane grabs my hand and pulls me to a couch that is sitting against the wall backstage. She just lets me cry on her shoulder as I blubber nonsensical words while my body tries to purge all the emotion.

It only takes like five minutes, and I feel so much better. I'm ready now. I take a deep breath. Karsten comes over to fix my makeup. Zane keeps everyone away while I gather myself. I feel like what I imagine my favorite actors feel before they're about to step out of their dressing rooms to perform, and a sense of euphoria engulfs me. I hold onto my new ring like it's my source of power and think to myself:

Remember that this is not about you. It's about all those people out there who might be helped because you told your story. It's about hopefully getting through to the Jessas of the world so that they stop being so GD mean to everyone, and it's about being an example. Just get up there and do your best. That's all. Just do your best. You've come a really long way, and remember, you're braver than you think. I twirl the ring, thank Zane and Karsten, go up to Mrs. M and say, "I'm ready when you are."

She gestures to an underclassman, who walks out on stage to introduce me, and I take one last deep breath before walking out to the podium.

Chapter Forty-Two

Okay, here we go. The big blue velvet curtain lifts, and I walk out to the podium and put my journal on top. I run my hands across the lettering, feeling every bump and groove as my finger slowly sinks into the embossing. I open the book to where I've written out my speech. Even though I've practiced it so much that I have it memorized, it still feels good to have it there as a safety net. I look around at the gym where, less than a year ago, I thought my dreams were finally going to come true, and the fame I'd always dreamed of was within reach. I look up at the spotlight to see my family, remembering how proud they were when I hit that note at the fall concert. I hope they're even more proud of me now. I feel a tingling in my whole body as I think about this because, for the first time in my life, *I'm proud of me.* I've worked really hard to get to this place, and though the journey wasn't one I would choose for myself, I did it, and no one can take that from me. I take a deep breath and can see some people get nervous as if I'm going to have a flashback. I chuckle. "Don't worry. I'm not going to freak out. I'm just taking this all in."

Everyone lets out a nervous laugh as the energy in the room lightens. I look around for another second and notice Karen Kolby and her news cameras, along with people standing in the aisles. I smile as I catch a glimpse of Jessa, and I have a moment of hope that this might help her too. But I turn my focus back to the group in the front row, the supporters I didn't even know I had until I spoke up. They are my main focus, and helping them is all I care about right now. They are the misfits, the outcasts, the people who suffer in silence. A lump starts to well in my throat, and I know I need to get speaking before I get too caught in my head.

I take another deep breath and hear someone shout, "You can do this!" from the crowd.

It gives me courage, so I begin. "Did you know that one in five teens contemplates suicide? That suicide is the second leading cause of death amongst our age group?" I pause for effect and also so I can gather my strength in the hopes that no one notices how my hands are shaking. Think about those kids, Nif. The ones who think there's no hope. Speak for them. I have to gather myself because that statistic always throws me. "There are many reasons for that. Sometimes we feel like we don't fit in." I look to find Zane. "Sometimes we don't love people society has deemed acceptable. Sometimes we're a little too much for the school we attend." I look at Karsten. "Sometimes our parents put an enormous amount of pressure on us. And sometimes we have true mental health issues that require treatment and medication just like a broken bone or cancer would. That's why I'm here today.

"But, before I go on with my speech, I want to take a minute to say that no matter what your reason for feeling like suicide is the only way out, please know that it's not. There are so many other paths you can take. I'm going to share my path with you in the hopes that it opens your eyes to the fact that there are options for you. Last year, one of my best friends introduced me to this concept called aggressive optimism. You may see people wearing t-shirts. They're kind of hard to miss." I give a little laugh, and so does the front of the room. "It's basically the idea that you can overcome anything, but sometimes you have to be really determined to do it.

"When I first heard this idea, it was just something kind of neat to try when I wanted to get a job, but didn't have the money for a car yet or if someone was picking on me and I needed to remember to see the positive." I look over to Jessa and can see that her face is red, and she's sort of sinking in her seat. I think it's the first time I've ever seen her embarrassed. Maybe the tides are changing. I get back to it.

"Then the crash happened, and, y'all, it was really dark in my head. Like, all the time. I felt completely hopeless because I wasn't sleeping, and the amount of energy it took to try and find the positive, I just didn't have it." I pause to let that sink in and look around the room.

"That's when I had to dig in even more. I started analyzing the concept and figuring out what worked and what didn't work for me. One of the biggest challenges with what I was going through, the PTSD, was that things that had worked for me my entire life, like writing to-do lists or talking things out with my friends, didn't work anymore. I felt hopeless. But I'm lucky. I have a great family and two of the best friends anyone could ask for, and they didn't let me give up." I look down at my journal because I know without my family, Zane, and Karsten, I probably wouldn't have survived, and the idea of looking at them right now is just too much, and I know I'll cry.

"Instead, we shifted our focus. I had an experience with my treatment where my denial of the situation nearly killed me, so I realized the very first step to anything is acknowledgment. You have to acknowledge that there's a problem before you can figure out how to solve the problem. Does that make sense?" I ask the audience and hold my gaze on them until they start to nod their heads, and I feel good about moving on.

"Once you've done that, you need to be willing to explore different options for solving the problem. Like I said, the ways that used to work for me were not possible solutions in my current situation. So, you have to go through a lot of trial and error until you find something that works for you. It might take you a hundred different tries before you figure it out. And you're probably going to feel like a failure a lot of the time. But the old saying is true—you're only a failure if you quit. It's also important to remember that the thing you find that works today might not work tomorrow. But the key here is to never give up. When I was in the psych ward, I was introduced to another concept called a 'toolbox.' And, as silly as it seems, I have an imaginary one I go to. I visualize my toolbox—mine is a yellow, retro-looking, metal box with a silver latch, and it makes a rusted, squeaky sound when I open it. Yes, I know that sounds crazy, but it works. And every time I'm in a situation where I'm not feeling my best, I acknowledge what I'm feeling, and I go to that squeaky yellow toolbox to see what tool I've learned from the many doctors, fellow patients, and other humans I've been fortunate enough to meet. Sometimes that's taking a walk, sometimes that's taking a nap, sometimes it's talking to a friend, sometimes it's writing in my journal. It could be any number of things, but all those ways of feeling better are stored in my little yellow toolbox, and I continue to add to it all the time.

"I've found that combining the mindset of an aggressive optimist with all the tools in my toolbox is the best approach to becoming healthy and psychologically whole, most of the time. I say most of the time because no one can be happy or feel good all the time. If you think that's possible, you are just setting yourself up for failure. But I can tell you that you can be happy and positive most of the time. That is true and something worth working toward.

"Sorry, everyone, I just get going and get so passionate about sharing that I sometimes forget that not all of you have been here for what's happened this year. And some of you are probably thinking, 'How do I know?' And 'Why would I take life advice from a teenager?' These are fair questions, so let me explain. Most of you know my story, and if you don't, it's been pretty well documented, so you can look it up. I don't want to dwell on why. Instead, today, I want to talk about the healing part. In short, I was in the farmers' market crash at the beginning of the year. What I saw broke my brain. I didn't have a physical head injury, but my mind couldn't handle it and didn't know how to process all the death and destruction I witnessed, so I developed a pretty debilitating case of post-traumatic stress disorder or PTSD. This disorder left me unable to read, stuttering when I talked, forgetting basic words, and having flashbacks and panic attacks daily. On top of it all, I wasn't sleeping. Eventually, I ended up in the hospital where I attempted suicide. I just didn't see a way out. I was one of the lucky ones, though. I had a lot of help. After all that happened, I was able to get sleep and begin to heal. I learned many, many tools, all stored in my little yellow toolbox.

"I learned how sleep affects my ability to function. And, as the person at the slumber party who prided herself on being the only one to be able to stay up all night, this one was a hard pill to swallow. I learned not only that, but how my diet affects my mood, how moving my body makes my anxiety less severe, how journaling about my dreams and hopes," I hold up my journal, "is as important to me as journaling about what I'm going through in the moment. I learned that for me, medication is important, at least in the short term, and that doing art calms my mind. I learned that taking care of myself is not a selfish act and that no one's feelings need to be hurt if you create a plan for when you're having a bad day.

"Needless to say, I learned a lot. Being in the hospital also taught me that what works for me doesn't work for others, and there's a million ways to do anything. So, if I can leave you with one lesson to hold onto, it would be that the key is to find your own way. Commit to having an aggressively optimistic mindset and then work to figure out a way that works for you. We're all different, and that is beautiful. You're worth the time and effort it will take for you to find your happiest self. And, since this journey is not an easy one and there are so many different ways to go down the road, I'm starting a podcast where I talk to other people who have overcome challenges. We'll talk about how they did that so you can fill your own toolbox and find a way that works for you. Let's commit to helping each other not become one of the statistics."

I grab the microphone. The size and feel of the microphone feels like an extension of my body and grounds me as the cold metal cools my warm hand.

I take a breath and look around the room at all the faces, some smiling, some crying, some contemplating. I soak it all in. *Well, this is it, Nif. Your last performance of your high school career.* I feel a tingle start at my feet; it makes its way up through every cell in my body. I nod at Mrs. M, and she gets ready to play. I open my mouth and sing the first three lines a cappella with a confidence I've never felt before. No red face, no nervous sweat, just pure joy as the rest of the choir comes out from behind the curtain carrying individual candles. The lights dim as Mrs. M begins to play a soft melody. The choir sings soft oohs in the background as I continue, "These candles represent the teenagers in this room who have contemplated suicide. We want you to know that we see you, and we are so glad you're here. Please reach out if life is ever too much. We love you."

Mrs. M gets louder on the piano as we all begin to sing at full volume. The floor shakes from the vibrations, the energy in the room is palpable, and I have this feeling that I just can't put my finger on when I realize it's… fun. I'm having fun. Like, more fun than I think I ever thought I could have. And I don't feel guilty about having fun, which is something totally new to me. I make note and decide to process this in my journal later. Right now, I'm going to enjoy the moment.

The song ends, and I am sweaty, my heart is pounding, and I am so happy. I hold in the bowing position just beaming with pride in myself. I can't believe how far I've come. I hang there for a few beats in silence when all of a sudden the ground starts to shake. I can feel it build up to my feet like a wave. Then comes the deafening sound of more applause than I can comprehend. I lift my head to look at the audience and see people crying and cheering and smiling, and I can feel a sense of belonging unlike any I've ever felt. It's not just that I belong; I can feel that other people feel seen and heard and like they belong. I truly feel like I made a difference, and I don't quite know how to process it, and I think, *You don't need to process it right now. Just enjoy it. This is literally your dream come true. Take it in.* So, I do. I wave and beam, and then, like Mrs. M taught me, I exit graciously. On my way off stage, I lock eyes with Jessa. I'm expecting an eyeroll, but instead I get a smile and a little nod of approval. *Did I just see what I think I saw? Oh, Nif, you don't always have to question everything. Just go with it.* I nod and smile back, and in some strange way, I know, Jessa won't be a problem anymore.

This time when I get backstage, as if out of a movie, the same stage hand that fell in front of me at the first concert is there. He congratulates me, this time with a tear in his eye. I can feel that he is one of the people I was speaking for. I take that in and say a really heartfelt, "Thank you."

I realize and internalize for the first time the idea of it not being about me. Like, I just happen to have a skill. I enjoy implementing that skill, sure, but the skill is just a tool I can use to help others. This whole thing isn't about me. It's about them. It's about making sure other people feel heard and understand that they're not alone and that there are ways to heal, to create lives we want to live. I turn back toward the stage as the rest of the choir begins to perform the next song. I take a deep breath and allow myself a moment to take in this accomplishment and lock in this feeling before heading back out to finish the concert when I hear, "Niiiiiiffff! That was just spectacular." I turn to see Karen Kolby walking toward me, her cameraman close behind. "Nif, wow. I didn't think you could perform any better than you did in the fall, but you just proved me wrong. Do you think you're up for doing the show?"

I pause for a moment fighting back fear and realize that fear is not real. *Going back to where the tragedy happened doesn't mean all the awful things I've gone through are going to happen again. This is your dream. Say yes! But she wasn't very considerate at the beginning. You don't have to like her, just remember it's not about you. It's about what you can do to help. If you have a platform you can use for good, you better dang well use it!*

I look up to see a confused look on Karen Kolby's face. She is definitely not used to people not asking, "How high?" when she says jump. I giggle a little in my head. "I'd be honored, Ms. Kolby. Is it alright if I call your office on Monday to set it up? I have to get back out and finish the concert now."

I can tell she's a bit taken aback by my newfound and hard-earned—if I do say so myself—confidence. And, honestly, so am I.

"Sure." She sort of half smiles with a little look of confusion showing on her face.

"Great."

I give my body a little wiggle as I think, *Okay, I could get used to this feeling.* Is this what confidence feels like? *I like it.* I walk back on stage, enjoying my life more than I ever thought I could.

The End

Acknowledgements

Making this book happen was a decades-long journey on its own and definitely would not be here without the loving support of my husband and soulmate, Craig. Thank you for being so patient as I worked through all that happened after the crash and then the various incarnations of this book. I love you and am so incredibly grateful I get to spend my life with you.

To my parents for all the lessons. Without you, I know I would not have had the strength to get through all that I went through, to learn and to grow from it. Your examples of making things happen live at the core of who I am, and I am ever so grateful.

To my sisters for making my life more interesting and fun. You inspire me daily.

To my brothers for just making me laugh. I can't tell you how much I appreciate that.

To my nieces and nephews, as cheesy as it sounds, you are the future, and I'm so glad. You're all such kind, thoughtful, wonderful little humans, and the world is a better place because you're here.

To my grandparents, who I am so lucky to have in my life.

To the incredible Polding family for being a shining example of what love and support looks like.

To Monica, who was the first to suggest I write a book about my experiences, your thoughtful encouragement was a guiding voice in my head throughout this entire experience.

To Cynthia and Shelby, without whom I would most likely not be here today. Thank you for helping me find the help I needed and making me believe I deserved it.

To Judy, thank you for making writing a book seem possible.

To Joy and Jamie, thank you for always being so encouraging.

To my business bestie, Katie, thank you for always being available for a verbal processing session.

To all my friends past and present, especially my "creative and chosen" family: Sally, Barbie, Jeremy, Jenn, Tyler, Sarah, Malia, Lynda, Katherine, Monique, Andrew, Lauren, Matty, Lindsay, Steph, Daniela, Dawn, Glenn, Kerrie, Kate, Michelle, Nina, Sami,

Alice, Kelsey, Tia, Angela, Popcorn, Tally, Michelle, Emily, Megan, Stephanie, Ilana, Molly, Yoko, Shirley, Neal, the entire Inspire-Impact sisterhood, Alicia, Cathy, Steve, Phil, Laura, Nicole, and, honestly, anyone I've ever had the pleasure of experiencing this crazy ride with. You all inspire me daily and are constant reminders to never give up the dream.

To Mary for going into "overachieving work mode" for me.

To all the medical professionals who helped me heal.

To all the "helpers."

To the entire Paper Raven Books team, you all rock! Especially the team who helped bring this dream into reality: Morgan, Rachel, Charlotte, Christine, Heather, Brian, M.A., Lynessa, Brianna, Brandy, and everyone working tirelessly behind the scenes. Special thanks to Colleen for the countless hours helping me to actually get the book down on paper and for making sure I was on track with my tenses.

Cover design by SamArt.

To all my ARC readers, your willingness to support me has been overwhelming and humbling.

To all of you, for reading it. I hope this book inspires hope and meaningful conversations that will help you through the ups and downs of life. You are more worthy and resilient than you know, and I'm so glad you're here.

And, last but certainly not least, thank you to Amy and Dominik, the two people who taught me what the term "chosen family" really means. I can't imagine my life without the two of you, the laughter, the hugs, the "fake argument" I know is going to happen because I put Amy's name first (it's alphabetical for the record). There are truly no words to express how much our friendship means to me.

About the Author

JENNA EDWARDS IS AN OPTIMIST, SURVIVOR, AWARD-winning producer, and bestselling author. She has previously contributed her stories of overcoming PTSD and mindset work in the books *Women Who Inspire* and *Moments That Matter.* Jenna believes we all experience things so we can learn and grow and shares her passion for Aggressive Optimism™ through writing, speaking, and podcasting. She lives in Los Angeles, CA with her husband Craig.

You can find out more about Jenna and learn how you can join the movement at www.jennaedwards.com.

Free Gift

Thank you for buying *Aggressive Optimism*.
Want to know more about the story?
Just scan below or visit the link,
sign up for my newsletter, and get a copy of
Will You Stand up?
The True Story Behind Aggressive Optimism.

GRAB YOUR FREE COPY

willyoustandup.jennaedwards.com